PACIFIC EMPIRE

PACIFIC EMPIRE

G. Miki Hayden

G Miki Hayden

JoNa Books
Bedford, Ind.

ISBN 0-9657929-1-9
Library of Congress Number 97-068452

First printing January 1998

To Lee Lozowick and Jace Walsh Szallies
with profound admiration and deepest appreciation.

Acknowledgments

My thanks to my publisher Perry Joe Glasgow, a man of intelligence and integrity, and a good friend; to my buddy Dennis, always my greatest reader; to my sister, Susan, for being an understanding voice on the other end of the telephone line; and to many others, such as our talented designer Eric Snyder, documentary artist and masseuse Lori Strober, and all my online friends who have shared the terrible burden of genius unrecognized. Heh heh.

Never the Twain

Fusako-san herself packed his traveling case for him, a token of her wifely duty–such symbol as he no longer cared about except as a matter of the traditions of their class. Certainly it was for form's sake alone that she performed this ritual, and as a sign of her allegiance to that which the Baron served–the Court and the Emperor. Sovereign Japan constituted the world that had given rise to Fusako and all that comprised her personality.

"Will you want your kimono and yukata in Germany?" she asked in the same impersonal tone that for 26 years she had used to punish him–although for what he did not know.

One of the younger maids stood by, eagerly assisting her mistress and fetching the Baron's garments for Fusako to place carefully into the suitcase.

"Whatever you choose," Baron Shimazo responded without thought. He sat at his desk, dipping the tip of his pen into the inkpot. He was writing a letter of instruction for his steward to execute while the master was in Germany. There was little, however, that Shimazo could add to the smooth and automatic running of the household and of the estate in general. The dicta he formatted for Tanizaki were a matter of correctness only, as Fusako's current actions were.

Shimazo's eyes slid once again to the woman at her task. Her presence in his private quarters irritated him and compounded the headache that already threatened to ruin his meeting with the Emperor. He felt invaded.

Invasion. It had, in fact, been during Japan's incursion into China in reinforcement of its Kwantung Army garrison at Mukden that the headaches had started. Shimazo had lain awake at night in his cabin on the *Maru Jintsu* off the coast of Korea (the gateway to Manchuria) assailed by the boom, boom, boom of the big guns firing their warning on mainland Asia. Shimazo had called on the

9

ship's doctor nearly every evening to prick him with his silver needles. "Kidney and spleen," Dr. Shinoda declared regularly, heating musky-odored moxibustion over the metal threads protruding from the Baron's skull.

The storming of Harbin not long afterward had exacerbated Shimazo's pain. Nerves, he had thought in all honesty. A samurai, a nobleman such as the Baron was, ought not react to the pressures of the situation.

Dr. Shinoda, no doubt to save Shimazo the brutality of the truth–and through caution lest the aristocrat turn on him–refused to comment as to anything of the sort, but the Baron presumed that his own conjecture was the reality of it. The slender probes inserted into his flesh did nothing to relieve his relentless condition, and once ashore in Manchuria, Shimazo ceased to call on the physician's feeble skills.

Although the Baron held the title of Colonel in the Imperial Army, he served solely as strategic advisor to Prime Minister Konoe Fumimaro, Prince Konoe, an old friend of his from the Peers School. The dispatches containing Shimazo's reports and recommendations went by pouch and plane directly to the Prime Minister in Tokyo.

"August 1931, Mudanjiang. A third day of heavy downpour, and streets and highways turned to mud have surely contributed to the mood of the troops, which translates itself into behavior beyond civilized description," Shimazo had written in one of a series of stiffly worded, severely critical communiqués.

"Our commanders have not lost control of their subordinates, as one might presume on viewing such scenes (as I have described in detail previously). I cannot imagine that, subsequent to our assuming control of this territory, we shall be able to rule easily a people so brutalized. Even the horse in the stable, badly whipped by his rider, may buck rather than cantor when next mounted by him-with-a-too-heavy-hand. I advise that the government send word to Yamashita (via Matsuoka, who has much power here) to quickly call his soldiers to heel. Otherwise, we may meet with a future, smoldering opposition even from this much-beaten donkey, which we now conquer so easily."

Truth to tell, Shimazo did not greatly care for the sights he encountered daily in the streets–the grime-encrusted children with fear-pierced, deeply-anguished eyes; the wizened ancients crouched in their rags and lamentation, abandoned homeless along curbsides and waiting to be trampled by the enemy.

Shimazo ignored the banging in his head as he tried to tear his gaze from what so commonly presented itself in front of him. On one occasion as he was about to seat himself in the jeep sent from headquarters for his use, a half-crazed woman ran into the street from one of the courtyards, virtually howling in her desperation. Shimazo, so generally stoic in his response, allowed a spontaneous distraction at her approach. Almost as if he had no awareness of the abnormality that they lived with every day, he followed the supplicant back into her dwelling where a Japanese soldier, his pants around his ankles, lay on top of a young girl.

"Get up, get up," the Baron commanded, banging on the man's back with the walking stick he carried about. These filthy, classless men from the farmlands represented his nation. How atrocious!

At the sound of an order barked out in his native tongue, the man half twisted away from the girl in confusion. The polished maple knocked heavily against him once, twice, three times. He leaped up, grabbing at his trousers.

"Good heavens, what have you done here?" the Baron cried. The rapist was Etumi, Shimazo's personal servant, now tugging up his pants. Shimazo indicated Etumi's way back to his quarters with the stick, then turned for a last look at the girl while her mother hovered over her. Shimazo strode out. Not even a girl, he decided, but a child, the blood flowing down between her thighs, a contorted expression of grief on her face.

Such an image ought not to have distressed Shimazo, of course. It would not have caused his ancestor, the feudal lord of Satsuma Province, to turn a hair.

One could speak of war and conquest in theoretical terms, but when a man–even one brought up to consider himself

11

a warrior—was faced with situations so different from the cozily domestic ones to which he was accustomed, there would be an effect. Shimazo felt ill and the pulse hammered away at his brain. The single thing he, with his all his training as a samurai, could do was to ignore the pangs of his own conscience thump, thump, thumping at his cells.

It wasn't even several weeks later when Etumi, bringing the Baron a pair of freshly polished shoes, halted before putting down the footwear, his eyes dropped toward the ground like a beaten cur's. Shimazo had not said two words to the man since that particular morning.

"Yes?" Shimazo demanded impatiently. The Baron was doing his duty, and thank goodness. Someone must represent the virtues of the Japanese Empire here, the inner stringencies and traditions that would prevail long after the vulgar trappings of this period of expansionism had died away.

"You must help me, Colonel," Etumi whimpered. "You must tell me what I should do."

Shimazo waited for the man to speak again. Truly he didn't want to hear, didn't care to know what the problem was. The exact same age as the Baron's son Hiroaka, Etumi stood in total contrast to that other young man's grace, education, refinement, and manly capabilities.

Little by little, the story came out in Etumi's stuttered and ill-chosen phrases. Who taught these men their Japanese? The young woman—the child—that Shimazo had found Etumi assaulting was by no means the first. *Perhaps it had come to be a form of addiction or sport for the valet*. But Etumi had paid for his crimes with more than Shimazo's cane against his back. One of those women had given him the dripping clap. How could he save himself?

Had they been in Tokyo, Shimazo would have liked to have seen Etumi taken out and shot. But they were in Manchuria, and Etumi was by no means alone in his sense of adventure. The raped, beaten, maimed, and swollen corpses of men, women, and children lined the streets of the town, unburied and festering, inviting some plague. Who was left to bury the dead? Who had the courage?

Etumi's life must not be wasted here, where the soldier had come to serve his Emperor and his people. Nor must the man be allowed home to spread the fruits of his depravity to a decent wife–as so surely he had infected that beautiful young girl...

Shimazo nodded and waved his servant away from him. Half-dressed and still barefoot, he seated himself to write to the cousin of a schoolmate, the commander of a battalion on its way north to Qiqihar. Etumi would carry the note to Tojo and the devil take the rascal. The conscript was posted to a front that saw two dozen casualties or more on a day's march. If he survived to return home–not likely–it would be without a limb or limbs. This was the best that Shimazo could do for all concerned, and so be it in the hands of their ancestors, the gods, or whoever, whatever, dominated man's fortunes.

"What time will the car come for you?" Fusako asked. Since Shimazo would leave for the airport directly after his meeting with the Emperor, Fusako would, as a matter of course, see Shimazo off at the gate. Appearances were the primary reason. Her husband must never be left with a nuance about which to complain, or a thought in his head that his wife was any less wellborn than he.

Shimazo affixed his seal to the note he had written and stood. "Are you done?" he asked, beginning to untie his kimono, a move that pushed the two women onto their feet and toward the door. Fusako rose swiftly from her knees, still graceful although well into her forties. "I'll have my bath now," he added curtly. "I leave at three."

Prime Minister Konoe had sent a Rolls Royce limousine to fetch the Baron, and Shimazo leaned back somewhat relaxed after his scalding bath and a rubdown from one of the maids. With pleasure, he inhaled the still-volatile leather upholstery. The

Baron had attended Oxford in his youth and had learned to appreciate a goodly number of things English.

There were many among Shimazo's circle who elected to follow the French in the all-important matters of comfort and style, but such was not the Baron's preference. The English opted for more than a little luxury, it was true, but there was also something spare and contained in the culture with which Shimazo identified, and that he chose over the flamboyance of the French conventions.

Still and all, though he was not a Francophile, it was a matter of pride to the Baron that in addition to an almost wholly accurate English, he spoke French. Von Ribbentrop, the man with whom Shimazo was going to meet in Berlin spoke both tongues fluently as well.

But it was not "Von" Ribbentrop, really, was it, after all? It was *Ribbentrop* only; the man, reared among the common classes, was a poseur. Shimazo smiled slightly to himself. The German Foreign Minister's plebeian background would surely simplify Shimazo's dealings with him for either one of two reasons. If Ribbentrop had an arrogant, inflated view of himself, Shimazo could easily command the man through manipulation of his ego. On the other hand, Ribbentrop might, unconsciously even, bend his knee to those he saw as being above him in rank, as was a Baron, even one of Japanese descent. Obviously Ribbentrop had some respect for the upper class, or he would not have taken on the title of "Von."

Baron Shimazo had been given a locked metal briefcase that held a number of confidential documents concerning Japan's negotiations with Germany. This case was beside him now in the limousine and Shimazo retrieved the key from his pocket to open it and refresh himself on some details he might need to discuss later on today.

Shimazo was a man of great precision and he knew in exactly what order he had replaced the papers in the case. Reviewing the contents of his files now, he ascertained beyond a doubt that he had not been the last one to peruse these secret notations. Suddenly, Shimazo felt chilled and sick again. Someone had been riffling through restricted documents while they were within his possession!

The significance of his failure struck Shimazo immediately. There could be no rationalization. The question of whom he must ask to aid him in his disembowelment flashed through his mind. Hiroaka, his son, would be man enough and the next Baron. The current Baron, still shivering, broke into a light sweat, and he began to plan the execution of his apology before the Emperor. This was exactly what he must do at once. Obligation to the Emperor was his first responsibility.

Seemingly simultaneously, Shimazo's racing thoughts took into account the diplomatic interactions with Hitler's Reich, once Shimazo was gone. Who would take over where he had left off? This would surely be a setback to the negotiations. Shimazo was uniquely situated to confer with the Germans, and they were prepared to receive him shortly—within hours. The Baron pulled a pristine white linen handkerchief from the breast pocket of his Western business suit and wiped his face. Other than this one sign, there was no outward manifestation of the turmoil within. His headache had returned, however, with a vengeance.

The only conclusion at which he could arrive was that he must delay his self-sacrifice and live on until, if suitable, these two nations had been brought together in an accord. Considering the greater good, Shimazo must give up the immediate fulfillment of his family's honor.

A deep shame at once swept over him. He must face his peers and his Emperor with this burning corrosion gnawing at his heart. His most urgent wish, which pressed at his temples, was that he not have to continue his existence one moment more.

The chauffeur pulled the Rolls to a halt at a side entrance to the Imperial Palace and Shimazo set himself to the business at hand. He was not a hotheaded boy. He could carry on despite his personal agitation. Once again touching the handkerchief to his face, he got out of the automobile.

He knew the Palace and was known here. Greeted first

15

by a Chamberlain who led him onward, Shimazo was saluted by the guards, one by one, as he strode along. His breathing had eased and he knew that he appeared entirely composed.

The Showa Emperor Hirohito received the Baron in one of the suites of the palace furnished in the Western style. The dark resonance of the rooms echoed the more traditional settings within the official residence. Shimazo bowed deeply in obeisance. All his life he had known this man before him, first as a young prince and then as the absolute ruler of Showa Japan. By absolute, of course, Shimazo meant in the moral sense–in reality the Emperor's power was held in check by the Meiji Constitution, which gave him reign in the military domain, but placed restrictions on his autonomy in affairs of state.

The Baron responded to Emperor Hirohito in the constrained, ancient language of the Court. Then the two men, together with Konoe and Minister of War Hata proceeded with a less-cumbersome, present-day Japanese.

Emperor Hirohito was stern–as if Shimazo had never heard these ideas previously. "Our small but mighty nation must expand. The remainder of the Twentieth Century will find us with a growing population requiring land. We must have Lebensraum, as the Germans say. And beyond that necessity, we have a Divine Imperative to unite all Asia into one single sphere. This is what the Americans once called their Manifest Destiny. It is our Manifest Destiny to yoke together the Asian realm."

Each man, still standing though the Emperor, a god to them, sat, nodded in somber agreement with this sentiment. Shimazo, in fact, concurred wholeheartedly. Japan must extend its influence and was superbly qualified to do precisely that. Beginning as a collection of feudal states that were characterized by frequent internecine disputes, the nation had successfully unified. History marched on. The same could be accomplished throughout the region.

There was one significant difference in Shimazo's opinion, however, from Konoe's. Their divergence was not one of ultimate aim, but of strategy. Two views existed among the

16

ruling politicians. There were those who believed that Japan must maintain and extend its hold in China, then continue on into the Soviet state, and those who felt their thrust must be to the south. Shimazo strongly believed in the southward drive.

Go oceanwards, Shimazo urged; next, consolidate those gains. Then, later in the century, Japan would turn to the north again. Shimazo believed he held the long view. The others were hungry more for their own glory and reputations than for the goals set them by the Emperor.

The Baron did not push his point too vigorously. Some concessions would have to be made to an ally's ambitions. If Japan were to join the Reich in common bond, Tokyo might agree to harry Russia on its eastern flank.

Dropped at the Hotel Brandenburg in Berlin by Count Asano, Shimazo found himself at a loss. His reason for not staying at the Embassy was a personal and valid one, but he should have thought to bring a manservant with him, at least to disperse his personal effects about his rooms. He called down to the desk and asked them in English to dispatch a maid to unpack his belongings. Since the hotel was a good one and used to an international clientele, the reception clerk understood his request, and only minutes later came a knock on the door.

"Come in," barked out Shimazo. He had removed his jacket and tie, and sat at the desk making notes on his meeting with the Count, who was stationed permanently in Berlin. The Baron had mixed a powder for his aching head.

He heard a rustle behind him and turned slightly to observe the German maid who had entered. The girl's brown hair was arranged tidily in a bun. Her sad, amber eyes indicated a certain level of refinement.

"Good day, sir," she said to him in a nearly unaccented English.

Times were hard in Germany, he knew. Well-brought-up young women must have been driven to take these types of menial jobs. "Good day," he acknowledged. "Please place my

17

clothing in the drawers and have my other suit pressed. I'll leave this one out to be pressed tomorrow morning."

"Yes, sir," she agreed. Apparently her command of English was quite good–a strong hotel English, in fact.

Shimazo had received some Deutsch Marks from the Count for use here. He took the packet from the desk and beckoned to her, then counted some bills and placed them directly into her fingers.

"Thank you sir," she said, watching him warily as she took the tip.

His hand retreated, his eyes fixed on hers. A woman in such a position must have many offers of money from men, all with implications that a female of good family would not appreciate.

And, indeed, the girl seemed glad to turn away as she began placing his apparel into the bureau drawers. He smiled as she took a hanger from the closet and studied the kimono Fusako had chosen for him.

"Put that in the drawer in its wrapper, just like that," he instructed. Folded along its seams with care by one of the maids at home, the dark-blue kimono, summer-emblemed with a geometric series of designs, would be suitable for wearing to the Japanese Embassy tomorrow night.

Shimazo returned to the questions he had pondered alone in the car on the way to the airport and accompanied by the deafening roar of the plane's engines all the way to Germany. Where had he placed the locked metal case at every minute it had been in his possession? And who had access? Shimazo's memory at fifty was not quite so flawless as it had been even the year before, but there was little that he missed in the moment, or could not go back and recreate.

Certainly the only location in which the case had been out of his sight for even a second had been at his chateau. That fact made the solution of this puzzle both more and less problematic. Shimazo could not even say that he knew every singe human being who lived on his property. Many were as familiar to him as his own family; they had worked for his father and he had known them since birth or since his youth. Others had been hired by his wife or his steward, and while a face might be vaguely known, the name escaped him.

What a shame! The domestic situation certainly had not been like that in his own father's time. The old Baron well knew the biography of every breathing soul under his dominion. Shimazo was stung by the thought that in yet another way he had failed to retain the good habits to which he had been bred. For so many flaws, so many sins such as these, so many inadequacies, his hara kiri would be sufficiently justified–if he needed more reason than the mere dereliction of his sacred duty.

"Is there anything else that I can do for you, sir?"

"Bring me a tea. "

Not many men and certainly no women would dare to spy on the Baron or on state secrets in the Baron's house. A lord in his manor still held the respect of those who served him. As for the one who did not carry him in such esteem–Shimazo's wife Fusako–she would very definitely not have touched the case. She would never have violated that boundary, even if all that had been inside were a flyer from the tailor he patronized in London's Saville Row.

Despite the hot sunlight beating down on the Kurfurstendamm, Berlin seemed dark. The tattoo of the soldiers' boots along the pavement made it so, first during the parade review to which Hitler's Foreign Secretary conducted Shimazo, and later, as they drove in an open car through streets thronged with men in uniform.

Berlin, it was true, reminded Shimazo of London, although the two cities were very much unalike. Both, however, were so utterly dissimilar to Tokyo that Shimazo was forced to connect these great Western capitols in his mind. There were other threads between the pair, but only later was he able to analyze his sense that something disturbing was at work beneath the surface.

As it was, Ribbentrop, or Von Ribbentrop, as Shimazo quite scrupulously called his host, was effusively welcoming. The Foreign Minister treated Shimazo and the Count as if they were old friends of his. Von Ribbentrop addressed them, and the undersecretaries who accompanied them, in English, occasionally switching to a sort of merchant's French–as Shimazo who had been tutored by a French Marquis considered it.

Von Ribbentrop was proud of the regime's military display, shrill in his enthusiasm. "One hundred-thousand men today, trained and ready; tomorrow, one million in uniform. The Reich has organization on its side–organization and discipline, and the Aryan intellect and virtues to make the Chancellor's vision a reality."

"A fine fighting machine," agreed Count Asano in all sincerity. The Count's retinue swung their heads rapidly in acknowledgment.

Shimazo smiled. The clap, clap, clap of what seemed like two hundred thousand boots stomping simultaneously against the sizzling pavement had given him a headache.

"Now for lunch," cried Von Ribbentrop. "You are my guests at the Rienzi. And I have arranged for the finest of French wines. Not too long from today, Meinen Taueren Herren, our countrymen will be toasting one another from the Palais de l'Elysee in Paris."

The feeling of discomfiture that had nagged at Shimazo came clear for him that afternoon as he stepped into the Hotel Brandenburg and the eyes of all in the lobby swung toward him in astonishment. He was as much an anomaly in Berlin as he had ever been in London. His face was unacceptable to them in the West. Or not his face, but the associations that came along with it. How well he recalled...while at school in England, in Oxford...the many slights...slights to the son of a Baron, bound to be a Baron himself. Slights, when he held so much of their awkwardness, so many of their inadequacies as individuals and as a culture, in contempt.

He had told his son, when Hiroaka followed his father on to Oxford nearly twenty years later, not to expect too much of the English. But Hiroaka, fortunately, had been a different matter. He was a soft, charming, and outgoing boy–well, now a man. He had made friends among the British aristocracy in a way that the Baron with his stiffer, more rigid personality never was able. Shimazo was glad for the child–genuinely so–relieved, in fact, that the boy had not had to face those surprised expressions, past which Shimazo now found himself marching.

As a man, the representative of one great nation to a country vying for significance (in Shimazo's view); as a Baron, the descendent of fabled feudal lords; as the master of an estate and a nobleman of wealth, his reaction was not the same as it had been when he was at university. He was no longer discomforted by their stares. He was angered! If *he* judged himself unworthy, it was not the same as *being judged* by them.

Approaching the concierge desk, Shimazo asked in English for the maid who had served him last evening when he had arrived.

"I'm sorry, sir, but that young woman has been dismissed. I will arrange to send you someone else." The matron behind the counter responded politely and without expression.

That was a point of interest, certainly. The maid whom he had considered so alert, so efficient, so competent had been let go. In these cases, he presumed, it meant that the girl had been a thief. This was an unexpected turn of events.

"Not for stealing, I hope," Shimazo remarked obliquely. "She unpacked my bag last night in my room."

"Oh, no, sir, not for stealing. You needn't worry on that account. We have none of that here. The girl is a Jewess. The hotel couldn't keep her on any longer." The mask cracked slightly. "Too bad, I suppose. Where can they go, I can't imagine." The head bent away and she reached for the phone. "I'll summon another maid for you, sir."

"No, no, don't bother." He had spotted the girl, carrying

21

a heavy bag and walking slowly toward one of the rear exits. Her face was pale, wreathed in what he imagined to be misery.

He had his own problems, so perhaps he recognized hers. He had already outlived his time by more than a day. He was a walking dead man. Worse. He had brought a great disgrace on all his house, his heirs.

Shimazo hurried across the spotless floral carpet after the girl, once again past heads that swiveled as he walked by, past tall scarlet roses in a crystal vase, past weary, luggage-laden boys in gold-braided bellhop outfits. He remembered a story from his boyhood of his grandfather who had befriended a poor farmer. In a lean year, the nobleman had allowed the farmer to fish in his streams and to hunt for rabbits in his park. "Why do you permit a man of no standing to eat what is yours?" other men of his rank had asked of him. Lord Shimazo never had bothered to answer such criticisms.

At a darker time, when Lord Shimazo's house was at war with a rival clan and soldiers had crept into Lord Shimazo's woods, the farmer whom the daimyo had befriended risked his life in making his way to the Lord's residence. He revealed to the master that the enemy lay close by and how many there were.

"One moment, Miss," the Baron rasped to the maid as softly as a voice accustomed to command could manage.

She did turn but adopted a posture meant to fend him off. She wanted nothing more to do with him. She desired to slink into the dark and to lick at her wounds.

"Since I have not brought a personal servant with me and as you are free, I would like to engage you for the several days that I am in Berlin. I will require nothing arduous or that a woman from a good home would find unacceptable." He spoke rapidly so that she would hear him out. "You will sleep in the antechamber to my room and can consider yourself under my protection. Do you agree?"

He might need someone who could be trusted with one task or another. There had been a Chinese boy in Manchukuo whom Shimazo had employed as a source of intelligence.

The girl didn't utter a word of response, but nodded, and he led her back into the hotel proper and to the elevator, which they then entered. The concierge's features formed again into a studied facade as Shimazo watched, but he detected underneath a moral outrage and distaste.

He had the maid draw his bath and lay out his kimono. After a while, he emerged wrapped in a towel and requested her to massage his neck. "I suffer from headaches," he explained so that she would not misunderstand his intentions. There were callouses on the young girl's fingers, a worker's hands.

As he lay under her ministrations, his mind worked away at his fixation. Who was the infiltrator in his own household? His steward Tanizaki might in any instance have entered his private study; no one would have remarked on it. Tanizaki came into the residence any number of times during the day to examine the books, even to take small amounts of cash from the safe. He was privy to every secret of the house, every nook and cranny.

But he was trustworthy, too. He had position and prestige. Why would a man throw all that away to rummage through documents that no loyal Japanese would have a reason to view? Perhaps Tanizaki was being blackmailed by the faction whose interests ran counter to Shimazo's–those who supported storming Asian Russia.

Shimazo had no disagreement with their final goal–the creation of a Japanese Empire that would rival that of ancient Rome–but he had seen war on the continent from a close vantage point. He knew the countless men the fighting had consumed. Japan's troops were not infinite in number. Even though a closer alliance with Germany might strengthen the Japanese position (Shimazo here underlined the *might*), that did not guarantee a single soldier more for battle.

The phone rang. It was Ribbentrop. How annoying! The Baron waved the maid away. The suite was not so large, however, that she would not hear every word spoken anywhere in it. Shimazo switched to his somewhat painstaking French.

Ribbentrop was merely eager to assure the Baron how

warmly Herr Hitler greeted Emperor Hirohito's emissary, how Der Fuhrer admired the Japanese people in their determination to establish an Eastern Reich. Hitler, in fact, looked forward to meeting with the Baron and would be available to do so tomorrow morning. Ribbentrop appeared exhilarated, drunk with his liege lord Hitler's approbation.

Shimazo uttered agreeable and meaningless phrases and glanced at his watch. It was not his intention to be late to dinner at the Embassy, but, first, he had hoped to have a nap. He allowed Ribbentrop to run himself down and finally terminate the conversation. The German people, no, the German commoners who had so aggressively taken power, were boors. For a moment the Baron felt entirely uncertain of the appropriateness of these negotiations.

Any ultimate decision about a concordat, however, would not be his own. He would return home with recommendations. Then whatever suggestions the Germans had made would be countered by the Imperial government in Tokyo. Next, several representatives of the Reich would come East. The Baron's work was only a link in the chain–but not an unimportant link. He laid the groundwork.

Shimazo called back his servant and asked for her name, absentmindedly still speaking French. "Miriam," she responded without requesting a translation of his question.

Ahh, what had he said on the telephone? Nothing of importance, anyway. Not much could be said to that blithering dolt "Von" Ribbentrop.

She was a girl of education; that was to the good.

The Oxford of 1912 was picturebook perfect: a gingerbread town paired with a university setting of heavy-granite dignity that somehow caused Shimazo to ponder how his own forebears had lived. This was a foreign place, but now in his fourth year at Merton College, he took some comfort in it.

Shimazo had never made up his mind as to religion. He performed the Shinto rites as a matter of course. The rituals were ingrained in him and in his family background. He might as well claim himself to be a Welsh coal miner as to not be part and parcel of a lineage that paid respect to the powers still extant of one's ancestors.

But his mother, a quiet and traditional woman who had grown up in a lesser-known Court family, was a loyal Christian inward and outwardly–though naturally still observing the better-accepted practices of their patrician culture. There was nothing that she wanted so much as for the future Baron and his sister Mitsuko to be Catholic, too.

He often seemed to hear her whispers in his ear, urging him to God and to the Church. Despite an instinctive, masculine aversion to following the leadings of the feminine–even those of a caring and nurturing mother–a shut-out, companion-starved Shimazo had begun attending services on the High Street more to be within eye and ear of other human beings than through some deep spiritual leaning.

It was unexpected that he should meet an English woman he could care for here. Kathy Larson was the daughter of a local bookstore proprietor and intense about her Roman worship. She took Shimazo to be as serious as she about their Lord, and he, poor lonely boy, did not dissuade her.

Miss Larson hardly seemed to remark on the fact that Shimazo clearly was not of England born. She was oblivious to everything but his radiant soul. And, in those days at least, the young man was not unappealing to the outer senses, once one looked beyond the unexpected almond eyes, the lustrous cocoa-butter skin.

Their love affair was consummated. Shimazo's upbringing did not lead him to be shy in any such respect. He had, of course, no intention of marrying the girl. He owed it to his parents and his heritage not to do so, but the choice was his to make, or it should have been. He was the one of a superior social class and financial extraction. She was from a line of merchants–good heavens, merchants!

Nevertheless, Eliot Larson, the father, made his daughter

break it off, causing a painful wounding of pride in the future diplomat. Anger and scorn spewed forth from Shimazo, but without an object, as he stalked the streets of that college town. Returning in the summer to Tokyo, he chose a bride, marrying the formidable Fusako-san, his "Iron Maiden." It seemed to Shimazo in some ways regrettable that he could not have been a grocer on Guilder's Green with Kathy Shimazo as his wife and three or four mixed-race, well-mannered English offspring.

The Mercedes sped them to Der Fuhrer 's Berlin residence adjoining the Reichschancellory. Ribbentrop, chattering anxiously at Shimazo's right, described the fortress home at Berchtesgarten that Hitler was now building, while Count Asano on the Baron's left maintained a respectful silence. Shimazo comprehended Asano's wordlessness far better than Ribbentrop's ill-suited preening. As a child, Shimazo had known the father of the Count. The Asano family fortunes had been failing even then, and had left the current Count with no choice in life but to seek his own way. The Asano estates had been all but swallowed up by a burgeoning, increasingly affluent middle class.

Hitler's personal residence was a hodgepodge of pretension. The Baron could not help but gawk in awe at the ponderous works of artistic mediocrity that decorated the drawing rooms. The nobleman had little appreciation for such things, but he had grown up, and had been schooled, among the finest of two cultures. Dutifully, he had paced past the portraiture in London's National Gallery.

Some of the pieces here, of course, were good by mere statistical happenstance. The Baron carefully suppressed a choking laugh, then glanced cautiously at the Count, whose eyes showed nothing but deference.

"A virtual palace," Shimazo remarked dryly. "Not unlike our Emperor's own." He had always considered himself an unrecognized wit.

Black-booted soldiers criss-crossed the rooms everywhere–couriers carrying vital messages, and appearing–in what for all intents and purposes was still peacetime–as if they were in the midst of war. "All decisions for the Reich come directly from Der Fuhrer," boasted Von Ribbentrop, regarding the dizzying scene with an attitude of complacency.

Shimazo and the Count gave their assent to the worthiness of such a scheme, although the two were from a social structure that greatly valued deliberation resulting in consensus.

Without pausing, Von Ribbentrop led the visitors into the dictator's living quarters and bid them rest in the straightback and comfortless chairs that served all waiting supplicants. Shimazo and the Count sat while the several others of their party stood formally–for all the world like samurai attendants to their Lords. And how could it be otherwise? Even these handpicked and able men were not in any way the equals of the Baron or the Count.

The Japanese did not speak among themselves as they waited, for in fact nothing needed to be said. Time passed–a great deal of time. Not a clock in the room, but the Baron heard the ticking inside his head, resounding like the steel toes of a thousand shuffling boots against brick paving stones. Shimazo's face turned red with the insult. He himself was immune from the sting of such a snub–a man who had not carried out his mission was beyond affront–but this delay was a patent offense to his Emperor.

A while later and Von Ribbentrop hurried out, an expression of anxiety disfiguring his face. "Der Fuhrer is not well," he murmured, advancing closer to his guests. "Nothing serious, of course. Nevertheless, he has graciously consented to meet with us. Here, I'll escort you, Baron, Count, perhaps the others will join us in a minute or two..."

Shimazo's body tensed at the peculiar invitation. A short century ago, a Lord Shimazo would have suspected treachery at such, and drawn his sword. But this was the Twentieth Century, and surely no similar meaning could be construed from Ribbentrop's request. Shimazo instructed their corps to remain and stood to follow Hitler's Foreign Minister. Count Asano rose as well.

The reason for leaving the others behind soon became apparent, much to Shimazo's immediate revulsion. The two noble Japanese had been invited to enter the German dictator's very sickroom. Hitler lay across a half-made bed, his suit jacket off, his hair dishevelled. A wet washrag had been placed over the ailing man's forehead.

"Der Fuhrer has a migraine," Von Ribbentrop explained into Shimazo's ear as they entered the Supreme Commander's presence. The Baron nodded in serious regret.

Herr Hitler had a migraine, had he? When did the Baron himself *not* have one? The last time Shimazo had been without a piercing pain in his head, accompanied by a wrenching at his stomach, had been days ago.

The German state rested upon this afflicted man's shoulders, and he lay on his sofa as the Pacific Emperor's envoys came to talk alliance. What an amazing sense of diplomacy!

"Mein Fuhrer," Ribbentrop began timidly, approaching the seat–no, bed–of power.

Hitler opened his eyes and pulled off the cloth, sitting up brusquely. His porcelain blue eyes penetrated both the Baron's and the Count's in turn. Each man bowed.

A rank odor drifted up from the couch to assail Shimazo's sense of smell. Unbelievable! Der Fuhrer had not washed in certainly days! With great effort, the Baron kept his hand from reaching into his breast pocket for a handkerchief to cover his nose.

"Setzen sie," Der Fuhrer ordered and the men pulled up two chairs. Shimazo had a little German, it was true, but hardly enough for a political discussion.

"We're so sorry to find your Eminence ill this morning," Shimazo began. Herr Hitler's title genuinely escaped him for a moment, but this designation would do for a man who clearly had no legitimate appellation. God Lord, though, he must try not to antagonize the dictator. "We beg your pardon for our intrusion."

28

Von Ribbentrop translated in some fashion or other.

Incapable of following Hitler's speech, Shimazo had the advantage of being able to simply watch the man. Sparks fairly shot from the German leader as he orated and the Baron fell into a sort of entrancement, from which he quickly roused himself. So, there was *something* to Der Fuhrer, after all! But whatever that *something* was filled Shimazo with a superstitious distaste that came both from his mother's Catholic teachings, which emphasized a fear of the demonic, and from his Japanese heritage with its countless stories of predatory ghouls.

The atmosphere that the Nazi warlord fabricated around himself was an unnatural one which made the ordinarily rational Baron think of hellfire. He had seen such supernatural flames before, of course–in Manchuria, where men had been turned into slavering beasts–and Shimazo had been certain even then that the Devil himself had held the reins.

"Der Fuhrer asks me to tell you how greatly he respects the achievements of your nation, your actions in China in particular. Japan, he says, is the Asian counterpart to our own Reich, an appropriate partner to foster world Fascism. We who reach out with force for what we want are partners with God in making history." Von Ribbentrop seemed pleased at his interpretation of the dictator's words, and in some way relieved to have spoken so well.

Shimazo had already sent Miriam twice to the Japanese Embassy to accustom her to acting as his messenger. She was timid though, and after pointing out that on the street she must wear her yellow star, she fretted that the Gestapo might arrest her. Consequently, the Baron had asked Von Ribbentrop to draw up papers that would allow his serving girl free passage throughout Berlin. Shimazo handed the *carte blanche* to her and took away her armband.

Tonight he requested that she carry a note from him to Ribbentrop and then wait in the servants' quarters for a response. "If you hear anything of interest, I would be glad if you would let me know," he added. He felt she already was aware of what she owed him. If not, she would learn, and later act as an observer where he himself was unable to go.

When she returned to him, her eyes were glittering. He didn't remark on it, but read the response from Hitler's Foreign Secretary. Von Ribbentrop was throwing a party to introduce Shimazo to the German elite. Elite, indeed! Shimazo decided he must wear his Colonel's uniform.

In dressing thus, perhaps he insisted on respect from these men, so wedded to their own forged-steel arsenal. If such a reaction were not forthcoming, Japan was better off without this consort. Memories of misuse by the British rankled. Yes, in London, he had met with their nobility, but that had been at his own embassy. Not once had he been included in King Edward's guest list. Not once! He, whose family had for a thousand years been an integral part of the Japanese Court.

"I did hear some things from the servants there," she told him, unable to contain herself any longer. "All sorts of gossip."

Shimazo gave Miriam a kindly smile and poured the girl a cup of tea from the still warm pot. He was pleased, very pleased, and waited silently.

"Minister Von Ribbentrop is off to Moscow in a week or two to meet with Stalin. The Russians are eager to see him also. They've tried to push up the date of the conference, but Herr Hitler didn't want to seem too interested." The girl was triumphant in delivering her news.

A swift fury rose up inside the Baron. In 1936, Germany had pressed Japan to sign an Anti-Comintern Pact to combat Communism and leave Stalin trapped with enemies on both sides. Now, even as Ribbentrop conferred with the Emperor's envoy, he was ready to fly off and sign a covenant with the Kremlin. Shimazo's cheeks burned. Any dealings between Germany and Russia would be a slap at the Emperor, an extreme humiliation.

"Was that all?" he asked, his voice thick with deepest emotion.

"Practically," the girl answered, unnerved at the change she saw in him, frightened by his anger.

The Baron stood and listened without prodding her.

"They say...they say...Herr Hitler has syphillis...they joked about it, but only a little bit. Someone else said it wasn't so, but that he was being blackmailed by Herr Himmler. He is sick, however. He shakes, they said." She waited, as if for the payment of a blow.

"Thank you for that," he responded in a subdued tone. "In time, I will reward you more directly. Now draw my bath."

Soon, ready and waiting for his car, he told her, "You see before you a full-blooded Aryan." He laughed as she gazed at him in puzzlement. "Yes, Herr Hitler has declared the Japanese to be full Aryans. In our case, the Nuremberg Racial Laws have been annulled." The phone rang, summoning Shimazo down to the street.

The following days were uneventful. Von Ribbentrop was solicitous of the Baron but involved in other details of his country's commitments. Having strolled Unter Den Linden and the Tiergarten all too frequently, Shimazo grew bored with the life of a tourist. He was ready to conclude their discussions and return home. A contingent of ardent German suitors would follow after in the fall; it had all been arranged. In the meantime, the keen edge of Shimazo's sense of dishonor had dulled–much to his dismay. He was eager to retire to his estate and to end his life while he still recognized the urgent need for it. Hot days in the European sun were putting him to sleep.

Were he later to visit Berlin again, however–as the thought flashed occasionally through the Baron's mind–he felt confident that he had a mechanism in place to aid his mission–his young maid. Miriam had been of some assistance to him in a series of minor matters, and should anything important arise, he felt he could rely on her totally. All that remained was to find a place for the girl in the meantime. Perhaps she would be safe running errands for the Japanese Embassy.

His illusions in that regard ended one evening as he sat jotting down details of a conversation with a deputy of Von Ribbentrop's. Miriam rested in an armchair by the door where he had invited her to settle and sew. Turning to gaze at her occasionally, he found that the sight of a woman at her needlework stirred an unexpected sense of contentment in him. The girl was a particularly intelligent and inoffensive creature who voiced no complaints, showed no undue expectations.

A sharp knock at the outer entry startled Shimazo out of his reverie. Ordinarily, he might have had the woman open the door, but he was bothered by the peremptory sound. He unseated himself and instinctively gathered his walking stick as he went.

Three German officers stood before him in the hall. "Yes?" he insisted, rapping out the English word.

"Wir suchen eine Judische Fraulein," one of the soldiers announced in tones more authoritative than the Baron's own.

"There are none such here," replied Shimazo haughtily. "No Jews at all. I am a guest of Der Fuhrer's Foreign Minister, Von Ribbentrop, and you have disturbed me."

Shimazo took an anticipatory satisfaction from this encounter. The walking stick in his hand concealed a fine sword and he was a trained and talented practitioner of kendo–the Japanese art of swordsmanship. He could, with ease, kill the three of them in seconds–and happily would–and get away with it too, as an honored diplomat. Thereafter, he might commit suicide and his act would be understood as a means of repaying the offense. His eyes shone as he imagined pulling out his surprise in defense of the girl whom he had promised to watch over.

Despite an apparent incomprehension of the English language, at the mention of Der Fuhrer and Von Ribbentrop, one of the officers bowed a retreat. Shimazo closed the door in their faces. His pulse was racing with an unfulfilled objective. He felt for a moment as if he could finally kneel down and draw a short sword across his abdomen.

When the Baron returned to the drawing room, Miriam was nowhere in sight.

"Come out, little girl, no big bad Germans will eat you today," he called expansively, resuming his seat at the desk in order to finish his work.

The girl emerged from his bedroom all atremble.

"When I leave Germany, you will come with me," he promised. She did not object.

A fiery strength appeared in his eyes. How weary he was, how angry at them all–at the English, at the Germans, at the spy in his own house. They had cozened him from start to finish, waltzed him around to their own tune. In turn, Japan would seize the southern territories from the British–even Australia might come under his nation's domination. In turn, the Showa Empire would not align itself with these Bedlamite Teutons. And as a final turnabout, Shimazo would catch the traitor inside his house and see him hanged!

That night, the Baron awoke to his own strangled cries of loathing and fear. Miriam, her hair down for once, came flying in to see what was the matter.

"It's nothing, nothing," he murmured, glancing at the clock. "Go back to sleep."

He was glad of one thing at that moment, very glad: He had not stayed at the Embassy with Asano and the others. Ever since Manchukuo, he often roused himself from sleep like this.

His sheets, when he lay down again, were soaked with sweat.

Not all of the notes that Shimazo had penned in Berlin were for official eyes. He had spent a great deal of time drawing up reports intended to mislead. That was for the benefit of the traitor who dared place his hands on top-secret documents of the Empire.

When the Baron returned to his estate, he left his case with the newly created papers locked but in plain view in his study. He paced about the house and grounds for the remainder of the week, waiting for the spy to take the bait. He was also eager for a chance to present the government with information he had uncovered in Berlin. Yet despite what the Baron considered to be the urgency of the situation, one could not meet with the Emperor without proper invitation.

Let there be no mistake about it, notwithstanding the articles Shimazo reviewed daily in the foreign press, Emperor Hirohito made decisions for himself. "The Emperor may not want war," he had read in a column in *The London Times*, "but he is led by his advisors and might not be permitted to intervene."

If the Emperor did not want war, there would be none; the Baron knew that to be the case. History might long debate the issue, but Shimazo understood enough about the Emperor to comprehend his power of personality. A shy man and a scientist of great intellectual curiosity, the Showa Emperor was nonetheless an individual of firm will and a sense of his position in the universe.

Emperor Hirohito had ratified the seizing of control in Manchukuo and applauded the prevailing tenet that it was Japan's divine destiny to dominate a Greater Asia. Shimazo concurred. The British had followed such a doctrine, far beyond its geographic base. Even weakling countries such as France and Belgium had legitimized conduct of that type. Hitler was correct in this respect. Far better to be the aggressor than the aggressed against.

Miriam had been settled in the maid's section of the house. Fusako-san, of course, must think that Shimazo had brought home a mistress. He feared that she would treat Miriam badly, and he urged the girl to come to him if she were bothered by anyone in the household. She was still under his special protection, he reminded her. She listened to him soberly.

"What do you want me to do now that am I here?" she asked. "Shall I work with the maids?"

Shimazo considered the matter. He must not set Miriam up too high or the other women in the house would knock her down. On the other hand, she was not suited to carrying out the normal tasks required in a Japanese domicile. She had no understanding of how things were done here.

"You will tutor my grandson," he answered at last. "Satoshi is five, and old enough to learn English and French." Then in a grave tone he added, "And you can help me investigate espionage."

Later, Shimazo called for his son, Hiroaka, and instructed him to have the boy ready to meet with his new teacher. "Tell Miako to cooperate. These are my orders." The Baron was more than mildly disapproving of his daughter-in-law, seeing her as a sort of Fusako-san in training. In time, she would pick up many more of the attitudes of her mother-in-law and make life as miserable for her husband as possible. The consequent effects on a household would not be good.

That led Shimazo to contemplate still once again whether or not the traitor within was Fusako-san. Perhaps she had been seeking out signs of his disloyalty to her and had mistakenly chosen to inspect the case with the official papers? That was an unreasonable scenario. Fusako had never interested herself in whether her husband had gone off with other women. She certainly would not care now that Shimazo rarely had anything on his mind other than politics or family position–or, more recently, the dilemma of when he might, in all good conscience, without harm to the Empire, kill himself.

Before much longer, Shimazo was summoned to a Cabinet meeting. He knew that there were those at the table who disliked him intensely, disagreed fervently with his point of view, and would like to see him out of the way entirely. But Shimazo did have the support of Konoe. Although the Prime Minister's government was somewhat insecure under the assaults of the extreme right-wing, Shimazo presumed that the coalition would hold while crucial decisions were being made.

Stationed at a lectern in the Western-style conference room, Shimazo faced the seven men who held in their hands the fate of Japan. Later, a complete report of the meeting would be made to Emperor Hirohito, who had undoubtedly read the Baron's preliminary adviso.

"Even as I stand here speaking to you," Shimazo began, "Minister Von Ribbentrop sits in Moscow drinking a toast to his Fuhrer with Josef Stalin. Hitler's government is conspiring to contravene the Anti-Comintern Pact that we signed with him in 1936. As Germany forms an alliance with Communism, it laughs in the face of the supposed friendship between our two nations."

Shimazo noted with satisfaction that although the Cabinet members had already read the account of his sortie on the Continent, which included this fact, their reaction to the announcement was nonetheless incensed.

"That alone would make any further alliance with the German nation unthinkable." The Baron emphasized his point by pausing to swallow some water from the glass in front of him.

"But I have a stronger, even more compelling reason for resisting too close an association with the Reich. Upon careful assessment—and I was shown many of the armed installations in and around Berlin and given intimate details of the military there—I can only conclude that Germany is not well-prepared for war. Its admiralty is in pitiable shape, with too few ships, inadequately armed. Hitler's predecessor, the Weimar Republic, was unready for another conflict, and Hitler himself is no better equipped. The German air forces are a little further advanced than the navy, but there are too few planes, of inferior make, and not enough trained airmen. We would be foolhardy to take on such a poorly situated partner—to link our fortunes with an impotent state."

The Baron poured more water and drank, allowing himself a moment of triumph. Everything he had said was true and could be independently evaluated by those who were present. They would only come to the same judgment as he.

He gazed most deliberately about at his listeners. "We, on the other hand, I am happy to say, have the greatest naval capacity in the Pacific. We have also trained more pilots in the last two years than in the whole of the decade prior." Shimazo did not point out that relaxing the standards for airman recruitment and education had been at his suggestion. He had seen in China the vital need for a strong showing in the air.

"Lastly, I must add my prediction that the German Reich will not prevail in any large scale confrontations. This is due to a political system that must, in the end, hinder its own functioning. I have seen with my own eyes the insistence of Der Fuhrer that he make every determination which in a smoothly running government and military must be made by the Prime Minister..." Shimazo nodded toward Konoe, "the Minister of War..." Shimazo acknowledged General Tojo, newly elevated to that post, "the Foreign Minister, and the Minister of the Navy..." He smiled vaguely at Hirota and again at Admiral Yoshida before naming the remaining Cabinet positions.

"Adolf Hitler is a sick man, dying, as they say, of syphilis. I well believe this to be true, having seen his leg tremble while he rested, and being witness to one of his hysterias. The man's disease has begun to eat away at his intelligence. Japan does not want to chain itself to a dictatorship dependent solely on its leader for all direction–when that head of state is losing both his mental capacity and his very life. Japan, gentlemen, is strong enough to strike out on its own!"

Yes, the Baron was making quite a leap in stating so conclusively that Der Fuhrer was moribund from syphilis. But Miriam had heard that rumor more than once, and Hitler's behavior at state functions could hardly be considered "normal."

Shimazo continued to stand and responded to questions. In trying to win approval to disavow Japan's association with Germany–or at least not renew or strengthen ties–he must not shift the emphasis by exhorting the Cabinet to veer from conflict with the Soviets and retrenchment in China. The rationality of his view would in time become self-evident. If Germany were seen as yoking itself to Stalin's regime, Japan would have to be alert to the danger of moving against this newly combined Power. The more obvious thrust for expansion would be to the south, where they could easily face down the weaker island chains.

That this progression would ultimately provoke Australia and its British progenitor was no secret to Baron Shimazo. That was a calculated risk and a not entirely undesirable consequence. A conflict of that nature contained more of a promise than a threat.

Australia's defenses would have to be assessed once the Philippines, New Guinea, and some of the other islands fell. Control of favorably situated territories would allow Japan greater ease of attack against that immense country's well-populated coast. What a prize Australia would be, although it might prove rather a large gulp to swallow at once. The Baron had many thoughts on that particular subject. He would like to show the West a thing or two about his people and their heritage, yet would maintain a caution in his dealings with Britain's heirs.

Would England spring to Australia's defense? Of course it would–if that were possible. Although Germany had tried to engage England in peaceful cooperation, such friendly moves had resulted in little encouragement–aside from Chamberlain's capitulation in various German offensives on the Continent. If Germany and England were to become entangled in a mutual conflict, that would leave the British with few spare resources for a counterattack Down Under against the Japanese.

Nor was the Baron afraid of intervention by the United States, a country that boasted a strong isolationist philosophy. The U.S. was neither well-armed, nor had any desire to involve itself in an international fracas not concerning its own direct interests. So long as Japan avoided hostilities toward that distant nation, it could expect no trouble there.

Today, however, Shimazo had only this first step in mind–breaking Japan's connection with the Reich and its lunatic leader.

The Cabinet seesawed back and forth in making its decision. Shimazo spent days transmitting urgent missives to those who had lent his recommendations their support. The defining moment arrived with the announcement in *The London Times* that the Soviet Union had signed a non-aggression pact with Germany. Thus scorned by its sworn confrere, Japan's governors determined to turn a cold shoulder to any further Axis courtship.

Shimazo was heartened by this new mood within the Cabinet, but he remained wary lest a reversal of that stance come at any time. He continued his frequent releases to the Prime Minister. And he added to the papers in his briefcase. Only days after Shimazo's return from Europe, the spy had begun dipping into the documents again.

The Baron was sickened by the thought of treason inside his own walls. Thank goodness he was aware of what had occurred and could control the flow of 'secrets' to the enemy, whoever they were.

He left the bait out, refreshed it regularly, and waited to snare someone, man or woman, for the executioner. Shimazo sought Fusako-san's opinion on international issues, hoping to trap her in an improper comment. But if his wife had any political leanings at all, she did not voice them. The only territoriality that seemed to interest Fusako was that within her immediate circle. Shimazo caught her watching Miriam like a peregrine intent upon a rabbit and again he asked the refugee to inform him if she were mistreated.

Soon, however, he began to observe that their Semitic maid had another source of solace. She was either very much taken with the Baron's heir, Hiroaka, or the young man was pursuing the girl relentlessly, without allowing her a refusal. Shimazo was not displeased in any way by this. Miako had not been his own choice for his son, and he approved of Hiroaka's taking his pleasure elsewhere than with the spoiled offspring of another Court family. Hiroaka must assert himself with Miako or the rest of his life would be miserable. Shimazo years ago had ceased to listen to Fusako's insults and complaints. Only that self-chosen deafness made his domestic life tolerable. He hoped that Miriam would offer his son some happiness.

Then came a day when Baron Shimazo realized he had too long delayed the inevitable. He was adrift, losing touch with any sense of decency and honor. Shimazo had made an effort to change the course of history and could bring no further pressure to bear. Each day he remained lord of his manor was another that cast a stain on his family honor.

The Baron would not commit ritual hara kiri after all; he would use his service revolver. He laid the pistol on a clean, white piece of paper in his study. The only misgiving he had was that he would spoil the room.

If he awoke on some fabled "other side," he swore to himself he would not haunt his ancestors' home. He would not want to frighten his grandson.

Ah, perhaps he had a single regret—that he would not live to see the outcome of his political maneuverings. If the country poured more resources into combat against Korea, China, Russia—the strong northern realms—such a miscalculation would sow the seed of Japanese failure. If another agreement were signed with Germany, the Reich would drag the Pacific Empire down. Yes, Shimazo had once had aspirations in regard to a Cabinet post...

The light rap on the shoji frame—her Western way of announcing herself—told Shimazo that Miriam had chosen an inopportune moment to have a talk. His long-delayed act would wait yet a little while longer. He invited her in.

Speaking English with her occasionally was enjoyable for Shimazo. He was also able to speak in English with his son, and soon his grandson, too. No, he was forgetting! There would be no *soon*.

She sat across from him, not looking up into his face. She was nervous, he realized. Then, seeing the gun, she startled. Shimazo slid the pistol back into his desk drawer and smiled. "In case..." he said.

"In case of what?" She was alarmed, imagining God-only-knew what prospect.

"Nothing, nothing. We're perfectly safe here. No need for

you to worry about a thing."

He immediately contradicted what he had just said by telling her, "If anything happens to me, I've provided for you in my will. So long as you're well-enough treated, I'd like for you to stay here with my family. But if one of the women bothers you, makes your life unhappy, Hiroaka will help you find someplace else to live. You'll have an income from my lands. Better than a lump sum, I believe. In war, the value of money may diminish." He felt that he had looked after many of the possibilities.

"What could happen to you? Nothing is going to happen to you, is it?"

"I've watched over your welfare," he continued, avoiding answering. "But I haven't been a real friend. I know that. I hope you've found a friend in my son."

"Yes..." Her face reddened.

"I never inquired about your family."

"I really couldn't speak of that," she replied slowly.

Shimazo nodded approvingly. Many things in one's life could not, should not, be discussed. People in the West rattled on too much from their egoistic points of view. The impact of events on individuals did not matter. No man or woman was singled out; tragedy, and comedy, happened to all. Shimazo had buried inside him, dealt with, many occurrences of which he had spoken to no one. That was an obligation placed on him by birth, a necessity that had strengthened him.

"Since my return home, I've been unable to find the spy inside my house. I will have to resign myself to this. That is what we're famed for in the East, surrender in the face of what touches each of us–life's realities. I have fought to make Japan a stronger nation, a greater presence in the world community. There's no passivity in how I've approached that task. But some answers are barred to us. I will die not knowing who the renegade was, only that I alone must be held accountable."

"You're going to kill yourself!" she exclaimed. Tears came to her eyes, as if his death mattered to her somehow. Her

41

emotion moved him.

"If I do, only promise that should you find the traitor you will see that he or she is stopped. If you can, that is, without risking your own position or your life."

She looked at him searchingly, a more intimate glance than she had ever shared with Shimazo. He felt stirred, almost in a sexual sense.

"If you knew who the spy was, would it matter? Would you then not kill yourself?"

"It wouldn't alter the disgrace of my failure."

"If the failure wasn't yours?"

"The deficiency is mine. I was entrusted with those documents." Her lack of understanding grated on him.

"If I tell you, you must promise not to turn him in or have him harmed."

"Don't speak," he answered harshly, rising. "Leave the room at once. Don't come in to see me again."

She stood, too, and held on to his Western-style rosewood desk, facing him fiercely, with the full force of her being. "Don't kill yourself," she insisted, as if she had a right to say such a thing.

He was speechless with outrage and waited until she turned and went, then slumped back down in his chair.

The conclusion was obvious, and for that reason, he had not let her continue talking. The one person who would have confided his guilt to her was Hiroaka, Shimazo's golden boy, his amiable, handsome, clever son. The Baron had been a poor father not to have transmitted the code of Bushido, of obligation to clan and nation. Their family was done for, gone. An ancient line had come to an entirely ignoble termination, with he himself the cause of its ruin. He had been too lackadaisical with his son, too moderate with discipline, too lenient by far. The sunny, chuckling infant had demanded it. The winsome child had prevailed. But he, the father, was exclusively to blame. He should not have allowed the many indulgences. His fondness for the boy had overridden his judgment as the holder of all his ancestors had established. Their very spirits screamed out at him. He had not done well and he could not now rest. What horror that a need for requital had, at the last minute, called him back to life.

That evening, before dinner, Hiroaka met his father in the English gardens by the pond. The young man, fit and muscular from daily romps with his martial arts trainer, stood awkwardly beside the gazebo bench. Shimazo signalled his son to take a place alongside him.

The Baron was composed, resigned to fate. He had been blithely unseeing as to the consequences of his liberalism with his child. For that, today he paid the price.

"Miriam told you," the son stammered out. "I wish she hadn't. But she has. It's not her fault, of course."

"She told me nothing," the father replied.

"Well, practically. Now you see what I've been doing."

"I see everything. I see nothing. I don't want to ask you a single question. Yes, one only, and answer me just yes or no. Do the British have the information that was in my papers?"

"Yes, but I..."

"Be quiet." Shimazo was pleased. The British had seen the plans and figures he had fabricated. That was very much to the good.

The son's eyes were anxious, remained steadfast on the father. "You'll want me to kill myself, I suppose."

Shimazo watched Hiroaka try to wet his mouth. "Is death so awful"? he asked his son. "All men must die."

"In time."

"Will it ever be time for the man who fears?" Speaking English, he wanted to use the designation "coward," but the explanation of such a word was many years too late.

"Father, what do you want me to do?" Hiroaka's eyes blinked closed.

"We have been at war in China and we are going to war elsewhere sometime soon. Is there no way in which you want to support your own nation and the Emperor?"

"But, Father, our side isn't the side of right. How is it that you aren't able to see? What gives us the claim to other countries' lands? What could confer legitimacy on such a venture?"

Ah, at least the boy had a rationalization for his actions and was not simply a sycophant, cultivating his British friends' goodwill.

"The English whose part you take and whom you admire so have done the same as this. Should the British flag not fly wherever the British people can enforce their will? Is it not fair that the stronger homeland with the more energetic culture rule?"

Hiroaka shook his head stubbornly. "Well, must I kill myself?" he questioned his father petulantly. "Is that what your sense of honor requires me to do?"

Shimazo lowered his head, observing the skillfully trimmed hedges, the well-weeded flower beds, the neatly manicured lawn. "You will receive a commission in the Imperial Navy," he answered his son. "I have written to General Yamashita, telling him of your wishes in this regard and of our pride in you. I informed him how eager you are to be involved and begged him to grant you a posting as soon as possible. You can use the next week or so to prepare yourself, or to flee to England–as you choose."

"I won't leave, Father. I'll accept your punishment." Hiroaka stood and walked away. Shimazo remained alone in the garden.

The boy had no concept of the consequences of his actions, thought Shimazo. How in the world could that be possible?

With Konoe on the way out after Germany's march into Poland on September 1st, the Baron was posited as the next Prime Minister. In that role, he might manipulate the nation's fortunes. By commanding Japan's forces south, he would win an almost unimaginable position for a country that was virtually a collection of large islands. The might of its consciousness would prove more persuasive than the prerogative of its size. How ironic if a soulless, irredeemable man such as he should stand at the helm of that dedicated national animus.

Hiroaka had been walking around in his naval uniform, bidding his goodbyes to schoolmates and family. Now he came to his father. He would leave for Yokihama this afternoon, by car.

Shimazo had believed himself a dead man from the heart out when he had discovered the violation of that with which he had been most solemnly entrusted. The sight of Hiroaka in uniform tore that still warm, beating organ into fragments. He felt to the core the loss of his son. Oh, too fragile heart, so captured by that long-ago little boy, surrendered to him so deeply that it could not recover and rededicate itself where it properly belonged.

Shimazo embraced that one-time innocence in farewell. Oh, Hiroaka was childlike yet. The father hoped against hope that the son would not die in the war–and that wish was a further treachery to his country's great lessons in manliness and fortitude. Shimazo was frail and had succumbed to an all-too-human nature.

Hiroaka pulled away from the Baron's unexpected gesture. "I'll do my best," he promised his father. Had he forgotten his protest against the Darwinian edict endorsed by Emperor Hirohito: "The fittest shall survive and, indeed, prevail"?

A little while later, as Shimazo watched from his bedroom window, the Mercedes pulled out of the drive with Fusako, Miako, and Hiroaka's own boy bowing their adieus. Miriam, of course–considered here as merely a servant–was nowhere in sight. Shimazo's still so vulnerable heart squeezed shut as the automobile swiftly disappeared from view. He lay down to dull a wildly throbbing headache with some sleep.

In the dead of night, as he tossed restlessly on his futon, he sensed rather than heard a pair of feet padding across the floor

45

to him. He turned and by the lanternlight reflecting in from the garden watched feminine legs approach. As she reached him, he pulled back the cover and allowed Miriam beside him. He held her comfortingly, soothing her as he would a child. Her seeking him out was flattering, but he was certain there was nothing to it more than a sudden loneliness.

As the moon rose, at her insistence, he made love to her. After all, Shimazo missed Hiroaka, too.

A Hot and Copper Sky

Captain Wakao slapped the new officer hard across the face.

The Captain wasn't angry, one of the sailors explained to Lieutenant Shimazo as he placed a piece of ice over his now-swelling eye. Wakao wanted to accustom him to life at sea.

The helpful crewman gazed at Hiroaka with a serious expression, trying to convey a further lesson to the young man, but Hiroaka was busy examining his visage as it reflected from a well-shined steel pan hanging in the galley.

"Arigato," Hiroaka thanked the kitchen worker who had doled out that precious sliver of ice, then he sought the stairwell leading down to the officers' cabins. He was outraged. He had never in his life been hit before, except for a light tap from his goju trainer. Wakao's stinging strike across the cheek and eye had been a grave shock to Hiroaka's system and he was churning with anger and self-pity both. He was ready to cry like a small boy, but held it in until he had closed the door behind him. Letting a few tears leak out, he took a handkerchief and blew his nose.

"Coming down sick already?" inquired a voice issuing from the bunk.

Hiroaka jumped. "What are you doing in here?" he challenged defensively.

"You don't think that you have a cabin all to yourself, do you?" came the amused reply. "This is my shift to sleep. If you insist on staying, you can try to be quiet."

Not even a room of one's own in which to think! The situation was inconceivable! Hiroaka wedged himself into the chair beside the desk and turned on the dim reading lamp. He had with him a pocket Shakespeare in an elegant gold- and amber-encrusted case and was intent on re-reading Hamlet.

Shakespeare had presented altogether an accurate portrait of a nobleman, he thought. But seeing how faithful the

Prince had remained to his father's memory made Hiroaka uneasy. Perhaps Hiroaka hadn't been quite as loyal to his own father as he ought to have been.

Young Shimazo was posted to the *Yura*, a five-thousand-ton Nagara-class light cruiser. Forced in 1922 to sign the so-called Washington Naval Treaty with the Western powers, Japan had many more light ships than heavy, in compliance with the specifications of that agreement. While technically in accord with the pact, however, these light-hulled vessels were armed almost beyond their weight capacity.

Hiroaka wasn't able to concentrate on his reading that well. The print was small and the light not sufficient; his cheek and dignity still throbbed. Yes, superiors routinely knocked their subordinates around in the military–he had observed some of that at the officers training school–but nothing of the sort had happened to him. No one had seemed ready to hit the Prime Minister's son. Perhaps Captain Wakao didn't know who Hiroaka was. Someone was sure to tell him and he would be all kindness and apologies.

There was a perfunctory rap on the door, which opened simultaneously. "Captain Wakao orders you up top," sneered a weathered seaman releasing his foul breath directly at Hiroaka who sat nearly in the doorframe, the compartment was so small. "You're on duty, if you haven't forgotten. He's not impressed by a Baron's son, you know. Barons, he said, don't have no ranking here."

Hiroaka's ire was again ignited. "Your name, man. What is your name?" he demanded.

"Sakano Joji," the smirking sailor replied with only a tad increase in cagey caution and respect. He slammed the door, causing Hiroaka's bunkmate to groan.

"I'm on watch in four hours," the sleeper grumbled.

"Don't mess with Wakao," he then advised. "He worked his way up from the ranks and has no liking for the upper classes."

What his cabinmate Miki had said, Hiroaka over the next few weeks found to be explicitly true. Wakao did care about Hiroaka's lineage, but in a way unanticipated by the younger man. The Captain enjoyed the idea of tormenting a Baron-to-be. And behind him came others—such as Sakano—who took pleasure in ragging an officer, so long as they could do it with impunity.

Sakano was low-class and filthy, if you asked Hiroaka. Of course no one on board was any too clean, due to a limited water supply—but some, like the Baron's son, knew how to maintain appearances. Sakano didn't even try. Hiroaka told Miki that the man had lice.

Miki, the child of a prominent Osaka physician, laughed. "They fumigate," he assured his raging bunkmate. "Sakano isn't as bad as he seems. He just needs some dental work."

Maybe Sakano wasn't as vile as he appeared, but Wakao was. Hiroaka learned to keep out of range when talking to him. But if Wakao reached to give Hiroaka a blow, it wasn't the young lieutenant's place to retreat or to duck. He had to take whatever Wakao chose to dish out. On one occasion, Hiroaka literally saw stars.

Hiroaka avoided writing home and whining—he knew his father would not appreciate complaints—but there were moments in which he contemplated suicide—more due to the humiliation than the physical pain. Hiroaka hated life at sea, and wished that he had fled to London as his father had suggested he might. He had many good friends there who would not understand such a life as he now led.

His eyes bleary from punishment and lack of sleep, Hiroaka tried to read a little of his Shakespeare every night to remind himself that he was a civilized and educated man. In the second week of his life on the ship he discovered, however, that this one material link with his past was gone. Stolen! The book and precious case had been a graduation present from his father. Damn the man who had taken it! May he earn his just reward!

Still, the days fell into a customary and almost soothing rhythm of little sleep, horrible food, and a good deal of wearisome standing in the salt spray of the Pacific. Had the war started? Getting news was difficult onboard the *Yura*. Hiroaka heard rumors, but no one seemed to think the seamen needed to know anything about what was going on in Tokyo.

Hiroaka was at the officers' dining table when, abruptly, his now-familiar–albeit uncomfortable–life changed forever. The sailors were commanded by the "all hands" signal to assemble on deck. Hiroaka swung himself up the stairs with adrenaline-heightened senses. Here was something to interrupt the tedium of life at sea.

With the crew standing at attention in relatively calm waters, Captain Wakao had one of his aides declaim a written pronouncement to the men. Hiroaka had the strange sensation that someone was about to read him a letter from his father. He attended alertly to what the news might reveal

"In the name of the Divine Emperor Showa, a striking force of six carriers, two cruisers, and escorting destroyers carried out a preemptive strike against the U.S. Fleet, which lay off of the Hawaiian Islands, poised to commit aggression against the peaceful Pacific Island nations. This precautionary raid took place on the evening of December 8th, 1939. Torpedoes dropped by an overwhelming force of Nipponese air power crushed the American battleships *Arizona, Oklahoma, West Virginia*, and *California*, as well as the aircraft carriers the *Lexington*, the *Saratoga*, and the *Enterprise*." The officer stumbled while reading those difficult-to-pronounce English names.

"Twenty-one warships and hundreds of aircraft at five American air bases on the island of Oahu were destroyed by the Emperor's unyielding and courageous forces.

"Two days later, on December 10th, a naval assault team led by Vice Admiral Nagumo Chuichi fully liberated the oppressed Hawaiian peoples from occupying U.S. troops. On December 11th, a provisional Hawaiian government was formed, and on December 12th, the islands and their inhabitants swore allegiance to the Divine Emperor, becoming members of the Showa Empire. "

Released by a covert signal delivered almost invisibly by the Captain, every sailor on deck of the *Yura* began suddenly to scream for joy, dancing and cavorting with his neighbors. Even the officers were caught up in the ecstasy, hugging their comrades and pounding one another on the back. All sailors joined in. That is, save one–a young lieutenant, who sank against the railing in a fit of dizzy disbelief.

This was not the message Hiroaka had expected to receive from home. Such a series of events as his fellow officer Ozawa had now related was, in fact, preposterous. Hiroaka's father, the Baron, would never have approved or permitted an assault against the American territories. The Baron's plans, which Hiroaka had himself read in great detail, had never suggested anything of the sort. To call the United States into the war at this point was contrary to every single national strategy advocated by the older Shimazo. Because of this certainty, Hiroaka was also convinced in his heart that his father was no longer at the helm of state.

Miki, who had tried to reach out for his bunkmate to slap him on the back, let his eyes flicker over Hiroaka with concern. "Get up," he hissed beneath the cacophony of the crowd. He tugged his friend to his feet and pulled him close. "People will think you're a Western sympathizer," Miki murmured, or at least that was how Hiroaka heard the words.

The young Shimazo began to weep. What fools his countrymen were to have started a war with the West. And it was all because...because, he believed...of a feeling of insufficiency on the part of Japan. Hiroaka's father (Hiroaka felt) nurtured such a feeling, too–a simultaneous admiration and detestation of the West. This, in the Baron's case, was due to the impression that he had not been truly welcome at Oxford when he was young. Damn it all! Damn it all to hell! Hiroaka's people had begin a war that was, no doubt, destined to crush them in the end.

He held the watch at eight o'clock that night. The *Yura* had been put on alert; the war had begun–they would not be caught napping. Hiroaka's eyes scanned out into the darkness aided by a powerful pair of binoculars. He knew that there were other vessels out there–two Japanese Yamato-class battleships, somewhat aft of the *Yura*. Those were not the objects he was looking for. He brought down the glasses to give his eyes a rest.

It wasn't until that moment that he noticed the Captain nearly beside him. Had Captain Wakao been so silent then? Or had Hiroaka merely been oblivious?

"No sign?" asked Wakao. Hiroaka couldn't tell if his superior seriously expected him to have seen anything so soon after the announcement of hostilities.

"No, Captain," he replied, wondering what the punishment was to be this time. He steeled himself for one of the Captain's pickish arguments, followed by a wrathful blow.

"Your father is dead, Shimazo." A smile played about Wakao's lips.

Hiroaka stared at the senior officer and nodded slowly. Hadn't he said exactly the same words to himself earlier today? Nevertheless, the news stunned him, and tears sprang into his eyes. Hiroaka and Wakao stood nearly toe to toe.

"I received a message to that effect two weeks ago," the older man declared with some satisfaction.

Hiroaka literally bit his tongue to hold back his retort. Wakao had known his father was dead and hadn't told him! Hiroaka was physically stronger than Wakao and most likely the better trained fighter of the two. He could seize the Captain and hurl him over the side of the conning tower. Hiroaka became a bit dizzy from both his self-containment and his deep, black thoughts.

"I didn't want the new Baron to neglect his duties," Wakao continued after waiting for a response that was not forthcoming.

Hiroaka turned away from his superior and propped the binoculars back over his eyes. Was there a speck far off to port? Was there something out there stalking them? He lowered the lenses away from his face. Possibly, just possibly there was.

"Nothing?" asked Wakao.

"Nothing," Hiroaka agreed.

Sakano marched up to the two men standing there. "Supper is served in your cabin," he told the Captain, all correctness. Sakano and the new Baron watched as their commander descended the stairs.

Hiroaka despised the seaman nearly as much as he did the Captain. As Sakano opened his mouth, about to tell the Lieutenant something, Hiroaka tried to predict what the man's next insult might be. Instead of words from the sailor's throat, however, Hell rose up from the ocean floor.

Confusion hit Hiroaka before anything else, as his world descended into chaos. The sea roiled beneath him. Then, sometime later, it wasn't below, but surrounded him, clutching him drenchingly in enveloping arms. He was not supposed to be wet. That's what struck him more strongly than any other impression his brain frantically tried to sort. He was gasping, soaked, but it didn't seem to be the time or place for such a sensation.

Once Hiroaka came to that conclusion, he realized that a mine had struck the ship, which was light enough to be sunk by a single well-placed blow. Still dazed, he began to swim away from the wreckage.

His father was dead and Hiroaka was in the waters of the Philippine Sea. This was a dream, a nightmare, and the shouts and moans he heard coming from the bobbing pieces of the *Yura* were only shadows of reality.

But Hiroaka was a strong young man and his body was unwilling to surrender yet to Owata-tsu-Mino-Kami, the ocean god.

An eternity of muscular charging through the salt sea led to an eon of floating on his back in some indefinable primeval soup that both chilled him physically to the bone and introduced him, finally, to stark terror. For a man to manifest fear was virtually

53

forbidden in the social milieu in which Hiroaka had his origins. Something in him tried to fight his panic, to return the lid back to the broken box. But phantoms emerged, demons in the shape of ferocious predators that tore at his flesh with enormous, grinning, lipless mouths; and bladelike teeth designed to rend. Vivid images of himself sinking beneath the ripples, unable to catch his breath, flashed through his head relentlessly. Hiroaka called upon his ancestors to spare him from this mental torture—not from the death that was inevitable. He groaned.

"Who is it?" came the startling demand from out of the black of pitch in which he dwelt.

Who was it? He himself had almost forgotten. "Shimazo," he wheezed out, rousing himself. "Lieutenant Shimazo." Baron Shimazo, he might have added.

"It's Joji."

Joji? Hiroaka pondered. Wasn't that Sakano's first name? He roared his laughter out into the vastness, nearly capsized with the outburst, then righted himself and began tiredly to swim again. What a beautiful irony! What a joke of the cosmos to give him an unscrubbed lout for a companion in death! But Sakano was washed clean now, although not free of the sores rooted in the man's low birth.

"I've grabbed a piece of the mess hall table. Come catch onto it with me. We can paddle toward land when the sun comes up," or so Hiroaka would have translated the man's thoughts into a grammatical Japanese.

Sakano wanted to drown him, Hiroaka supposed. The idea dissipated for lack of motive. Sakano wanted Hiroaka to help steer his "craft" to shore. Once there, they would be rescued by some native tribe, helpful or hateful toward the race to which Hiroaka and Sakano both belonged.

In the gloom, Hiroaka followed Sakano's voice and finally reached out, gripping onto the table. He had arrived once more in a country of men, of customs, of law, of objects with form, of relationships. A sort of ease came over him. There was security in this manmade thing. Like all stability derived from a human source, of course, it was delusory and fleeting. The hereditary Baron's intellect grasped that, but his body expressed its gratitude at succor in a sigh.

"We can sleep," he told his fellow traveler. "So long as we don't let go of the table."

The two men and their new-formed nation drifted on fate's tide.

The dream was that he was home with his son and Miriam, his lover. The three spoke English, as they soaked in an immense wooden tub. "The water's cold, too cold," objected the boy.

"It's a mistake, all a misunderstanding," Hiroaka soothed his child Satoshi. But what was going on? Wasn't he himself dead? Or was it Miriam who had recently died?

Heat and brightness descended from above, although the lower half of his body remained chilled. He clutched harder at whatever he was holding onto–then awoke. How absurd! Where was he? "Sakano," he grunted excitedly. "Look, look, over there. It's...something."

Sakano started to kick his legs to propel their island kingdom.

"Stop. Don't," Hiroaka fairly shrieked. "You'll attract sharks. Don't churn the water."

They made their way toward...whatever it was. After perhaps hours, Hiroaka let go of the table and began to stroke carefully through the waves.

"Wait. I can't swim," Sakano called out.

Hiroaka had to decide what action came next. Damn! He returned for the seaman. Together they made their way to the atoll that shined above the glittering Pacific, promising the men their very lives. The pair dropped the wooden plank near the shore, and Hiroaka dragged his compatriot onto the sand.

The castaways lay on the beach beneath the scorching sun, breathing hard. Finally, Hiroaka came to his senses, stood and waded into the ocean with Sakano shouting out to Hiroaka as if he had gone mad. After several attempts, Hiroaka snagged the table board and pulled it onto the bank. This was the sum total of all that which they owned.

But they possessed what nature had made for herself, as well. Espying a grove of palm trees further up on the land, Hiroaka urged Sakano to crawl as far as that blessed shade. They must not burn up in the heat nor dehydrate too quickly.

Water was the key issue here; that much was obvious. They could live without food for a period of time—certainly while exploring the tiny island for something to eat or for a Man Friday to teach them the local survival skills. But without water they would soon die, and painfully, their tongues hanging out, seeking to catch the least drop of moisture.

Hiroaka, who had studied English literature at Magdalen College, gazed out on that fabled "water, water everywhere," wishing that he had learned more sciences. There must be a way to filter the salt from the ocean's well! He tried using a piece of his uniform as a cheesecloth, but the results were putrid and he spat the liquid out.

"Clouds," he said a little while later, and in the sand on high ground dug holes as catchpots for a rain that might eventually fall. He ordered a grumbling Sakano to do the same.

With his one tool, a pocketknife, Hiroaka sliced a notch into a palm and planned to do so for every morning this sun rose on the two of them.

A useless task, Sakano told him.

The Lieutenant made Sakano empty his pockets so that he could see what else they had.

The only object of value the man had secreted there was that amber and gold case Hiroaka's father had given him, and which Hiroaka had so prized. He took the treasure into his own hands now and fondled it, then wiped the incorruptible metal against his trousers. Hiroaka opened the box and brought out the cherished little book to dry, placing the case into his shirt next to his chest.

Sakano eyed him curiously but said nothing—nor did

Hiroaka. The theft of the case was truly beyond discussion at this point. They were both going to die, but Hiroaka had his belongings back.

The horror of the situation struck him to his essence, yet he could not speak on that topic either. Hiroaka had been trained to leave such things forever unmentioned. The two men would expire, turn to dust, with none to mourn them here.

So be it.

After a long sleep, thirsty, of course, but somewhat recovering their strength, they paced this small, uninhabited island. They plucked the brown, ripe coconuts that had dropped from the palms and with difficulty shredded the husks, broke into the nuts, drank the milk, and fed on the meat. There were too few of these fruits to truly assuage their need for nourishment, but Hiroaka could feel the life pour back into him. Later, they could devise a means for fishing, while waiting for the rains.

"Parrots," exclaimed Sakano, pointing.

Hiroaka admired the squawking creatures dressed in festive green finery. That must mean there was water here somewhere.

"We can catch them and roast them," Sakano exulted.

Never mind that they had no matches, no fire.

Hiroaka was saddened. Yes, probably they should trap and kill the birds, but the thought sorrowed him. The galahs–or whatever species they were–belonged here. The Japanese sailors did not.

Only two days later, a storm rose up quickly out of the sea and descended violently upon the island. Hiroaka and Sakano set out what coconut shells they had for water, and held the ship's table between themselves and a wedge of a tree as the wild torrent battered at them. Hiroaka, who had yearned for a pure, fresh drink, and who now had all the water he required, was not pleased.

Strong as he was, the stress of the elements had been too much. By morning, Hiroaka had come down with fever and a chill. The flaming orb extending blazing rays toward him from a great distance above blinded his eyes and overpowered his effort to rise up and care for his most basic of needs.

"Joji." he whimpered.

Joji reached into the Lieutenant's already rotting shirt and removed the bejeweled case. "Since you're going to die anyway, I might as well have this," he explained. "It's worth more than I ever made in my whole life altogether, you know."

Hiroaka blinked in the dazzling sunlight. Joji went away, and a little while later returned. He fed the new Baron a brew of coconut milk and water.

"I couldn't catch any of those damn birds," he grumbled. "I've set a snare."

Joji took Hiroaka's hand, for what purpose Hiroaka could not at first fathom. Then Sakano pulled off the gold school ring that the nobleman wore. "I might be rescued," Sakano said, slipping the ornament onto his own finger. All Hiroaka could do was watch and tremble with the ague. When next Sakano gave him water, he threw it up.

That night, Sakano sat by him, griping about their situation, for all the world as if they were boyhood pals from the village of Sakano's birth. After his litany of objections at having landed on this blasted place, Sakano stopped short. Hiroaka began to drop off to sleep once more, wondering if he would awaken ever again.

"I've always hated men like you," Sakano said finally, interrupting Hiroaka's drowsing. "You've had everything that those of my type have not been given. And you've detested us for our base manners and impoverishment. You've drained us, taken the best that any of us had, and left us to do without–unprotesting." That's how Hiroaka heard Sakano's words, in a more comprehensible and literate language than the man actually spoke.

"But don't think that those of your class can discount the rest of us." Sakano grimaced in a sort of implied triumph. "We have our ways of getting what we want, of having our revenge."

"More water," whispered Hiroaka. "Wet my lips."

Sakano stared at the supplicant, but then in a moment carried out his companion's request.

"I married at a very early age," Sakano continued after a while. "I chose a woman who could be a help to me in getting on in life. She was no beauty, but I never could have provided for one who was. She was hard working and didn't talk back. Over the years, I became quite used to her and to her ways. We were a married couple as it ought to be—bonded so as to care for one another as men and women must. All had worked out for the best, and I considered myself a fortunate man."

Hiroaka coughed and began to shake anew. "If only we had a fire," he said.

Sakano got up suddenly and disappeared into the dark. When he reemerged some time later, he had fronds in his arms, which he piled around the sick man, creating at least the illusion of warmth. No, the palm leaves did trap in Hiroaka's body heat, although they did too little to relieve his chill. "Thank you," he told Sakano gratefully. He had not expected such consideration.

"There. I've earned the ring now, fair and square," replied the peasant-sailor, pointing at the object in question. Apparently the jeweled case wasn't worth mentioning. After all, Sakano had already owned that for a time!

Sakano settled himself again and shook Hiroaka, who was falling back to sleep. "I haven't told you my story yet. And as you might die tonight, you won't have heard it."

What difference that would make, Hiroaka could not discern in the slightest, but he fluttered his eyes open to indicate that he was listening. The water and the blanket of vegetation were worth more to him than a mere gold signet, so he added to that price his ear.

"After two years of marriage, Kitako and I had not conceived a child. People around us began to wonder at the problem and I was the butt of many a crude joke. What was worse, however, was that Kitako herself was greatly pained by our lack. She wanted a young one to nurture and to rear.

59

Certainly though our failure was not for want of trying.

"We consulted a doctor, despite our having no money with which to pay, but he sent us away, saying that he could do nothing for us. I didn't know whether that was because we had nothing to give him, or he genuinely had no cure for our difficulty.

"Another year went by without any offspring. I would have resigned myself to this condition, but my wife Kitako began to pine away. Then the means of making her happy sprang unexpectedly to hand, quite without my seeking it out."

Hiroaka had to interrupt Sakano's discourse at this point since, shivering and weak as he was, he nonetheless had to answer nature's call and couldn't do so on his own. Sakano assisted the Lieutenant in rising and took him off several yards into the dark. He helped his patient to squat and even cleaned him up afterward–although not without vocalizing his objection.

Hiroaka was enormously fatigued when Sakano returned him to his bed. Although the sick man had been willing to hear the other man out, a relentless tiredness forced his eyes to close and he slept. When Hiroaka awoke in the middle of the night, trembling and sick to his stomach again, Sakano was nowhere to be seen.

"I had taken an occasional job in those days helping the gamekeeper at a grand old estate in our prefecture. That is, when the gentlemen came down from Tokyo for a weekend in season, I was one of those who tramped out into the brush and scared the game into the hunters' path.

"I had no respect for those of wealth and rank, as I've told you, and on one occasion when I was given a task inside the mansion, I took the opportunity to filch a silver spoon from the kitchen. That was a boon to me and my wife as I sold it for seed for the next rice planting." Sakano looked delighted at the thought of his petty pilferage.

"In time I also made friends with a maid in the house–Honako–and spent some pleasant hours with her."

Hiroaka paused to cough, hacking up a great deal of phlegm. While the sun had warmed him, he was also sweating quite a bit, and knew he would readily become dehydrated. They still had water from the rain, but that would go soon and Sakano was not likely to share the very last with a dying man. Sakano eyed Hiroaka now, in fact, as if wondering how long his companion would last. Not wanting to leave his story untold, the sailor-farmer hurriedly spoke on.

"Soon, I knew everything of note that was going on inside that house. The mistress was in residence in the country now and was suffering from nausea in the morning. When I heard that news I was stricken by a jealous rage. How was it that a family who had money and power should also have the other great good fortune? You might say that I was beside myself, and in that passionate state, I hit upon a wildly clever scheme. Well, perhaps you will call it an evil idea, but given the circumstances of my life, it was the only possibility open to me.

"Yes, you may have guessed it by this time. I had Kitako present herself to the neighborhood as one who was pregnant. We kept her padded and put out that she was to deliver at such-and-such a time, the same approximate date, of course, as the Countess was due to birth her child."

Sakano paused a little, with a wicked smile, and took that moment to pour some coconut milk into the sick man's mouth. Though his stomach recoiled, Hiroaka swallowed and managed to keep the liquid down.

"Kitako protested my plan at first, you understand. She was afraid. Then, too, she thought perhaps it wasn't right to take another woman's infant away. But I convinced her. Or I didn't persuade her so much as insist that she do as I instruct her. Once we had the baby, she would be glad. Then, a few days before the child was due, I made Kitako stay indoors. I told the neighbors that she was lying-in and that I had called a midwife from another village.

"In the meantime, I went up to the estate and had my way with the maid there once or twice. ...If you live another day or so

I might want to relate those details to you...

"When the baby was born, the priests and well-wishers came, and the family was all smiles.

"I'm not a thief by nature or by birth, you understand, but by conviction. I believe that I have as much right as every other man to happiness. I am not a typical Japanese citizen, you might say. Somewhere along the line I lost my sense of place, my humility. I began to take what didn't belong to me and found that I liked it. Yes, I even enjoyed the act of theft itself by then. I felt a sort of fulfilled retribution in taking from those who had so much more than Kitako and I. And I had my ways of stealing things, you see. Such as when I took the silver from the kitchen.

"Kidnapping a baby was another matter entirely, as you might suppose. People watch out after the newborn ones. The little ones cry. There are all sorts of difficulties. Three days after the child was born, his wet nurse brought him to the servants' quarters and set him down preparatory to feeding him. Just then, she was called into another room. I had at that instant walked into the house and hadn't announced myself to Honako yet. This was the opportunity I had been waiting for, so I snatched up the boy in my arms and ran."

Having concluded the meat of his narrative, Sakano stopped speaking and lay down on a pallet he had fixed for himself not far away.

It took a very long interim for Hiroaka to work up the energy to open his mouth. "Then what?" he asked.

"Then what? Then nothing." Sakano turned onto his side and slept.

Hiroaka napped, too, waking up hours later to the dimming of the sun. Sakano was unmoving yet and Hiroaka croaked out to him, "Joji." No answer, but his breath rose and fell.

This was a dismal outcome of a life–a sort of perishing by attrition, with nothing meritorious about it, no room for an heroic stance. Hiroaka would just lie here and dry up like a sponge cast onto the shore. In the full length of time, only his bones would remain, bleached by steady rays of solar light, the swooping parrots having pecked his skeleton clean.

Sakano grunted once, sat up. "What time is it?" he asked.

Time was a forgotten concept. "Night," thought Hiroaka in reply without sound.

Sakano staggered over to his patient's couch. "I don't feel well," he whined to the other man. "I've caught your infection."

"A quick death," Hiroaka mumbled consolingly.

Sakano continued in a hoarse voice with his tale, exerting less energy in the telling than he had earlier. "Those damn stupid aristocrats had never paid attention to the villagers, of course. Our births, our deaths, our sufferings were invisible to them. Although they searched far and wide for the Count's missing son, that lost child was never found. Maybe some of our neighbors suspected what we had done, but nothing was said to the best of my knowledge. They were too afraid to accuse Kitako and me, or they had no more concern for the aristocracy than I.

"He was a good lad from the first, a sturdy, intelligent boy, a joy to behold.

"I had deprived Mitsuo of his class rights, but if there was any resentment on his part, he showed no sign." Sakano smiled sadly to demonstrate that this was, indeed, a deliberate `joke.'

"As the years went on, we forgot how Mitsuo had come to us and genuinely believed that he was ours from birth.

"Remember that I said that I was married young–and although my face may be lined, I am still not old. That is how I came to be drafted into the Navy. I wasn't unwilling to serve, you understand, for although I hate the rich, I have never been disloyal to our Emperor." A flash of patriotism signaled itself through the peasant's now feverish eyes.

"When I left home, the boy was 17. He's nearly 19 now and by the last picture his mother sent, a fine young man. We have given him everything that we were able. I have always wanted him to have a better life than I–though not so good as he was by heritage entitled. Yes, a splendid youngster, intended for a Count and transformed into a peasant's son. What do you think of that, Lieutenant, you being one of the nobility yourself?" Sakano's expression took on a malevolent, triumphant cast.

"What province?" Hiroaka questioned. "What family name?" From the start, this was what he had waited for Sakano to reveal. Hiroaka knew all the first families, of course, and could recall no tragedy of this type. But then he might not know the story of each and every lineage.

"Count Asano in Harima." Sakano's face was flushed.

Asano. Hiroaka had heard stories of the present Count, of course. His father had met with him recently in Germany.

His father was dead, Hiroaka remembered with a start, and Hiroaka's son would soon be the Baron. Ah, at least Hiroaka had left an heir for the title–an honorific he had so long ago–it seemed–broken faith with in stealing secrets for his country's chosen enemies.

"I must have a rest," Sakano announced, interrupting Hiroaka's musings. "We'll die together, you and I, and if they find us here, they'll take *me* for the Baron with this ring." Sakano rubbed Hiroaka's school symbol, shining it, as both men faintly, each for his own reason, smiled.

Joji was dead when Hiroaka woke up again. Once more, the sun had started to emerge. Unable to continue to notch the tree, Hiroaka had lost track of the days. He stared at Joji for a while, trying to detect the slightest movement–but there was none.

How inconstant of Sakano to die so abruptly! Hiroaka wondered how long before he followed the fellow's example. His mind began to haze with a dreamy melancholy and he heard only dimly the squawking of the parrots. One flew down and settled on the mess hall table.

She preened herself. Ah, what a beauty. If he could reach out and take her by the neck and strangle her, would he? Would he tear the flying animal in two to save his life? Hiroaka roused himself and attempted to sit up. No, he rose not to catch her, but because she reminded him of life. He desired to live. And, in fact, despite his circumstances, and even in the face of Joji's death, he was feeling better today. He stumbled to his feet and the bird flew off as he pursued her.

Surprisingly, moving about invigorated him. He didn't go too far at any one time, but stopped and recovered his strength along the way. This was a poor land for growing anything; he hoped he wasn't expected to claim it in his country's name. He laughed a little–to himself, of course.

There was an opening in a coral reef that led inland. Water had ponded here, but he couldn't be sure if it was potable or salt. A grass-green flutter of wings and Hiroaka's parrot friend–or another, surely–dipped a confidant beak into the pool and sipped. Hiroaka could drink here, then–and eventually, he did. There was enough fresh water for a while–after that, the rains might come again. He shuddered.

The bird didn't seem to mind the man's approach, although she eyed him with some perplexity. She didn't recognize his type, it seemed; still, he was not her natural predator. Perhaps he *ought* to make that meal of her. But then again, remembering his Coleridge and how badly the Ancient Mariner had fared after slaying the Albatross, Hiroaka stayed his hand. As if things could get much worse for him! Well, if he were destined to die, why sacrifice the bird's life, too?

Should he recover from his illness, there must be some way for him to survive. Perhaps there would be no purpose to it, to living alone on a deserted isle–but maybe he would do it all the same. He had his Shakespeare after all–with any number of plays still left to read. The first business at hand, of course, was to bury Joji. With no means to start a fire, cremation was impossible.

He would bury Joji with the ring. Joji had better than paid for that, and would sleep more comfortably in the hereafter carrying some fine possession with him. Hiroaka would retrieve the jeweled case, however. That was from his father.

He drank again. There might be ways to keep himself alive...

From the diary of Dr. Shinoda Tomoyuki:

December 23rd, 1939–Terrible news. Our sister ship, the Yura *is sunk. Many of the survivors, however, are being picked up by the* Musashi, *which had followed behind. Thank God for that–a Christmas miracle, for those of our faith.*

December 24th–Vice Admiral Toyoda invited me aboard the Yamato *to dine. I have been treating the Vice Admiral for some arthritic pain, but he is feeling none of that tonight in his exultation over further victories at sea. Moreover, he assured me, with the American fleet entirely destroyed in the assault on Pearl Harbor, there is not sufficient U.S. force to defend that country's coastline. I did not take it that he believes Japan's armada will move to carry our expansionist efforts to that shore itself. Rather, our strategy would be to use this as a persuasion for convincing the Americans to sign a treaty with Japan.*

The war, in other words, is going well.

December 25th–A few of the men on board the Natori *are Christians and we soberly celebrated this most glorious of days. I pray for the souls of our sailors who have been lost at sea and for the souls of the men whose ships we ourselves may sink.*

Toyoda said last night that the only country remaining as a threat to us in the Pacific would be Australia. The U.S. has practically committed itself to neutrality and Britain is boxed up in the North Atlantic. Still, the British could conceivably be so moved by Australia's imagined plight that it might send troops, even when it could not send ships.

January 17th, 1940–General Douglas MacArthur, stationed in the Philippines as part of an earlier American effort to coerce that country into an Anti-Nippon alliance, has been recalled to Washington. His troops have been withdrawn as well.

February 7th–We have heard that Philippine resistance is

collapsing and that we can expect these islands to join the brotherhood of Asian nations under the leadership of the Emperor.

February 23rd–Japanese troops have swarmed the Philippines. I am most certainly gladdened at the prospect of peace and a future prosperity for all our peoples.

March 3rd–The Natori *has joined a sweep of the small, outer Philippine islands to verify that there are no pockets of rebellion, so that the area may be considered secured.*

March 15th–Foul weather again. We are all eager to move on. According to the news from home, we have definitely signed an agreement with the Americans. All liberated territories, including the Hawaiian Islands, have been ceded to us in return for a promise of no future hostilities against the United States.

There is a great deal of speculation aboard as to whether the U.S. would remain out of the war if Australia were attacked, and whether we should pursue such an aim. I leave questions of that sort to the policymakers in Tokyo. They know the full scope of possibilities for our success in such a venture.

March 20th–These forays onto the tiny islands (comprised mainly of coral and sand) that dot this part of the world have taken on a day-to-day sameness that is boring for the men. Any objection, of course, is only that they cannot participate in a more active enterprise for their country. Daily we hear of skirmishes throughout the Pacific ending in victory for our side. Enemy bombers have flown out of Australia with some regularity, however, and there has been damage to our naval air forces upon which we so heavily rely...

April 8th–Something unusual today that brings a patient into my hospital. The men have returned from one of their expeditions with a Japanese sailor. The man, I am told, was quaking and hiding from their approach, and only when unable to flee stood and surrendered.

Poor fellow. He is terribly emaciated and still seems inordinately apprehensive. He will not speak, although I have assured him that he will be looked after and not harmed. I cannot understand how he got onto that coral reef or what he has to fear from us, his countrymen. It is a mystery that only he, in the course of time, can unravel. His uniform was ragged and showed the emblem of a lieutenant, but I do not think that a man of this sort could actually have been an officer. His eyes are haunted, so his tale will not be a pretty one.

My medic has cleaned up the man and fed him a cautious meal this afternoon. I would like to believe that we can nurse him back to health of a sort. Yet what he has witnessed and experienced may never be erased. That is often the case when a man has seen and felt too much in combat.

The Reciprocity of Tears

Mitsuo lay belly-down on the floor of the room he shared with Kawabata. He had brought a reading lamp from the desk there with him and was pouring over a set of maps. He had owned these particular maps since the age of 11, when he had first become aware of the fighting in China. One of those often-creased and somewhat tattered territorial delineations was of Manchukuo, but now Mitsuo had spread before him the entire world. As a boy, he had followed the details of the conflict in China by listening to the radio–exactly as he was doing now.

Not precisely the same. The war had recently taken on a greater dimension, swelling Mitsuo's pride in his country's martial spirit. Mitsuo was himself well on his way to serving as a warrior. He was in the midst of his training as a fighter pilot.

The young man studied the cartographer's drawings, trying to imagine his father, Seaman Sakano, out there, somewhere. The depictions Mitsuo was examining at this moment were of no use to him, really, because his father was currently far away at sea–not a location that was graphically differentiated from swell to swell. Mitsuo and his mother had not heard from his father for several months. Perhaps the older sailor had not found a willing hand to write for him again.

The Imperial Navy had been battling native troops in the Marianas since the withdrawal of U.S. forces there. The Americans had given up their interests in the Pacific in a formally-signed agreement with Japan. Although England, which governed such territories as the Solomon Islands, had denounced the pact, the United States had been leery of entering into hostilities with the growing Nippon Empire. Japan, in turn, remained circumspect about committing itself to actions against any part of Great Britain.

Perhaps Mitsuo's father was among an armada pounding at the British gates, riding the crest of the wave on a magnificently built battleship and staring down the enemy as he loaded a torpedo, or gazed up over the sights of his anti-aircraft gun...

"Where are we now?" Kawabata called to Mitsuo as he entered the room. Graduating from fliers' school a week from now, the handsome and gregarious pilot was an ill-matched roommate to the painfully taciturn and zealously intense Sakano Mitsuo.

"Say we had a base on Timor," Mitsuo suggested, referring to the map. "It's terribly close to northern Australia. With planes like the Zeros that were just delivered, it would be nothing to fly across the Timor Sea and take out some of the Australian air defenses." Mitsuo fell into musing over the colorful charts.

"You and I?" joked Kawabata. "Shall we take on the Australians?"

"I don't see why not. It's an awfully big chunk of land."

"All right. I'm game." Unconsciously, Kawabata took on a swagger as he headed across the room, and many would have thought his attitude all pose—unless they were aware that Kawabata would finish first in his class at the Navy Fliers School at Tsuchiura. He was fated to become an ace—as well as a popular leader of his fellow fliers.

Mitsuo was at the head of his own class, three months' behind Kawabata's, and for that reason the powers-that-be had tossed the two young men together to see what would come of the mix. Perhaps they thought the splendid older student would be a positive influence on the shy, socially awkward Mitsuo. But what they did not understand was that Mitsuo would scorn his bunkmate—as much for his offhanded grace as for his seeming lack of seriousness.

While their superiors saw Kawabata as the more promising of the two fliers, Mitsuo conceived of himself as the one who would be a true Japanese hero. Steady and alert, his dedication to homeland was complete.

70

A vision of a man's future may be entirely deceptive. No one can understand his destiny or another's, either before or after the fact.

Two days prior to his graduation, in a last training flight over Tsuchiura, Kawabata Kinsuke was dashed to the ground by mechanical malfunction of his Mitsubishi Type 96 and the forces of nature. His was the first death of his class, and at commencement a tearful father was awarded a silver watch from the Emperor. The memento had been intended for the most promising air pilot of the group—a tremendous honor.

Mitsuo couldn't have been more stunned by this sudden turn of events. Kawabata had been foreordained for so much glory; he had been so admired. His toothbrush still hung on the hook over the sink.

Mitsuo helped the father and mother pack their dead son's few possessions. Life here had been hard, even for Kawabata. There had been no luxuries. The officers were stern, often beating their students for the slightest mistake.

Mitsuo didn't have one single bracing or cheering word to say to the bereaved parents as they placed the few pieces of clothing into a small suitcase. He turned over in his mind the possibilities for a proper condolence. He wanted to comfort them, but Kawabata had died before fighting for his country—and therefore Mitsuo could not see that his roommate had succeeded in any way whatsoever. On the verge of achievement, Kawabata had been an utter failure.

As the dazed couple thanked Mitsuo, bowed repeatedly, and was about to move off, the boy stuttered his reassurances at last. "Kinsuke-san studied very hard. He caught more flies than any of us."

Mitsuo responded to the parents' suddenly confused expressions by making a fly-snatching motion with his right hand. Each of the pilots-in-training did his best at all times to improve his reflexes. Plucking winged insects from the air required speed of reaction and dexterity. Mitsuo was at a loss as to how to spell this out, and allowed the mother and father to depart without clarifying his point.

If Kawabata had died because he was too cocky, Mitsuo would take care not to imitate that attitude. Mitsuo, who carried a notebook of sayings around with him, made a note of that.

No one worked more diligently than Mitsuo. In the evenings, he placed a newspaper over the floor and practiced strolling on his hands. The more secure one's balance–even, or especially, upside down–the more apt he was to survive the maneuvers required in combat. That was not only personally important, perhaps a small matter, but he was a trained fighter, a defender of his nation and valuable to the Emperor.

The father, performing his duty somewhere in the Pacific, would be satisfied with the son's accomplishments. Mitsuo, like his classmates, was able to drop from a 20-foot-high tower to the ground and land on his feet. He could hang one-handed from a climbing rope for 15 minutes. There was almost nothing he could not or would not endure.

Kawabata's memory did not live on for long. He would have departed about then anyway, along with the others in his training section. A new cadre of students entered immediately after and Mitsuo had someone more his own type to share his room–a quiet and studious boy from Saga.

Because the preparation of pilots had been so greatly expanded several years before, about 200 airmen graduated from here every three months–compared with 100 a year before the fighting in China. That meant each trainee had to go a little further and drill a bit more fervently. Just because there were more airmen being turned out didn't mean that the control panel of the new Zeroes or the pilots of the Australian B-26 Marauders would be any more forgiving.

Something uncommon, but perhaps not too remarkable, occurred one morning when the cadets were in the yard half-naked, performing calisthenic drills in the cold. Vice Admiral Ota, the head of the academy, marched by with his 17-year-old daughter, Akiko-san, and two top officers unfamiliar to the men. The four looked at the troops intently, and as they passed Mitsuo an energy of recognition came into the eyes of the young girl. Of course she knew who Mitsuo was, he and Kawabata had crossed her path once as she bicycled into town and the two students were on their way to class. Kawabata had taken off his cap to reveal a striking headful of palmaded hair and had stopped the girl to ask her jokingly for a ride. He had clowned about, pretending to get on the handlebars while Akiko giggled frantically.

Mitsuo thought nothing of the inspection by the officers until he was called into Captain Junichi's office an hour later. There he was confronted by the sight of the Captain and two military patrolmen.

Mitsuo gave all a curious glance, then broke out into a nervous perspiration. Perhaps they had come to tell him that his father had died, or some other awful news.

"You are under arrest for rape," the Captain announced harshly. "I hope they place you in front of a firing squad. You are a disgrace to your uniform and to your service."

Giving Mitsuo not even a moment to take a breath, one of the naval police immediately shoved the flyer toward the door. To say that Mitsuo was in shock would be an understatement. His legs barely held him up as they removed him from the grounds.

"You ought to have gone to a prostitute," Niori, the airman who shared Mitsuo's cell advised him in the tone of one urging a beloved nephew to take some well-chosen action.

Mitsuo turned up his nose at the man in disgust. Mitsuo had not spoken to Niori after an initial few sentences. The youngster did not choose to associate with someone such as Niori–a man who had blatantly stolen Navy equipment to sell on the blackmarket.

"A girl above you–that was bound to get you into trouble."

Niori was full of tidbits of this sort, remarks of a kind that grated on Mitsuo, who considered himself to be a morally superior human being–an exemplar Japanese national.

"Or if you seduced her, you surely made her angry for some reason," Niori concluded. "Playing around with another woman?"

Mitsuo fumed.

Not in the least sensitive to emotional nuance, Niori nonetheless dropped the topic for a while. He had another issue on which he liked to harp–the flying he had done in China.

"I guarantee, we released bubonic plague on all three villages," he was saying now with relish. "You can't imagine how carefully they handled the payload when they brought it onboard. The sweat was popping out of them for fear they would crack the damn container. Anyway, I heard from some guys in the Army garrison in Zhejiang later on. They had to go back and burn a load of bodies and some of the houses. They had us do it as an experiment, I heard, but I believed they used it as a warning." Niori smiled. "Whole villages wiped out, I mean. Of course, you couldn't consider it any fault of ours."

Mitsuo concluded that the pilot was making up the story simply to bait him, and didn't answer.

Niori snapped on the little wireless that his wife had brought. Tinny, patriotic music sputtered out of the box. Soon, an announcer came on and began to deliver the news.

As Niori moved to change the station, Mitsuo called out curtly, "Leave it," between a plea and an order. Niori shrugged and pulled his hand away.

Mitsuo wished that he had his maps in front of him here, but he had studied them so well and for so long that he could see the outlines in his mind's eye anyway.

There was fighting this week in Sumatra and Java–the Lesser Sunda Islands, as it said on Mitsuo's map. The Japanese, of course, were winning–with heavy air support from Type I bombers. The bombers were protected by a buzzing nest of Zeros that swooped in to strafe after the Type Is had made their runs. Or so Mitsuo played the scene in his head. The lumbering bombers dropped their ponderous load onto a Dutch airfield decorated with unbroken lines of Curtiss Mohawks–P-36s. The Mohawks had been caught unaware and not a single pilot had left the runway. With smoke pouring up out of the damaged planes on the ground, the bombers headed back to sea, toward their own sanctuaries. Mitsuo in his Zero rushed groundward to strafe, as a Marauder, the last plane still standing in one piece, lifted off from the field and climbed in pursuit. Mitsuo's Zero rolled and twisted, his finger groping for the cannon trigger...

"Sakano Mitsuo," the guard called out. "You have a visitor."

His mother–after all, a mother!–was allowed to talk to him alone in a small private room. She sobbed so, he could barely understand her. Mitsuo held his head straight and stiff as he tried to soothe her. He was perfectly certain, too, that the sequence of events which he painted for her would come to pass. He would be back at Tsuchiura by tomorrow, or within days at the most. There had been a terrible mistake and any minute now the girl would come to her senses. She would realize that she had identified the wrong man. Mitsuo would soon be released.

This woman who sat beside him had borne him, had fed him from her breasts. And although he could not recall the time before he stood erect and began to follow his father into the fields, he felt he could remember the descent from her womb–he had been told so often of his birth.

This woman, his mother, gazed at him through tear-streaked lenses. "We never should have..." she muttered. "However we brought you up... This is our fault...our punishment."

Mitsuo could make no sense of what she said and he merely repeated his pledge to her that all would be well. The mix-up of identities would shortly be resolved.

His mother shook her graying head in despair–or, could it be?–in shame. For his entire life, each accomplishment of Mitsuo's had seemed to be the natural harvest of both who he was and his parents' admiration of it. Now, suddenly, his ears must burn that he had brought his mother to this pass.

"A miracle, too good to be true...." she whispered.

"I'll make you proud again," he promised. There was no doubt. No doubt at all.

Mitsuo's carefully constructed illusion vanished during an interview with the military prosecutor. Nakajima urged Mitsuo to confess so that the sentencing might quickly proceed. "You will want to save Miss Ota any embarrassment, of course," Nakajima insisted vehemently. "She's three months pregnant with your child."

The young man blushed to hear of it.

Certainly Mitsuo's image of himself as heroic archetype included a notion of the utmost courtly behavior toward all womankind. And Mitsuo genuinely had a kind streak in him. His compassion rose out of every indulgence that had come his way from a devoted female parent whose mothering had known no bounds. She had trotted after the toddler Mitsuo lest he falter and fall or stub a tender toe and wail. This had created in the boy a corresponding softness of heart.

Yet to confess meant to abandon his dream of circling that enemy airfield and homing in for the strike–or coming head to head with a Lockheed Lightning in a dogfight so heated that by the time he downed his opponent he would be drenched in perspiration and shaking with fatigue...the lot of an ace, but he would be humble. It was all devotion to country and Emperor, after all.

He came out of his daydreams to see that Nakajima was awaiting his answer. The noble samurai who Mitsuo had willed himself to be, modeled himself after, would say `yes, I confess. ...' But Mitsuo was in reality the son of a wily peasant, was he not? "I will think over what you suggest," he replied reluctantly. "I would like to spare Miss Ota any sense of grief, of course. But you see, I didn't...would never have..." he could not even utter those final, unseemly words.

Nakajima scowled threateningly at the boy. "I will come

again tomorrow," he rasped out.

Mitsuo frowned. His father, whom he often thought too severe regarding the upper classes, perhaps was correct. This Nakajima abhorred Mitsuo, thought himself above the pilot who had so diligently applied his efforts only to the good of his nation and to winning its war.

He lay on the hard wooden plank that served as his bed and pondered the right and wrong of it, while the radio announcer's voice blared between shotgun bursts of static.

Niori opened the back of the device and flicked his finger against a vacuum tube. "Might need replacing," he assessed. Niori was being moved any day now to a large prison in the south. He was lucky not to have been placed before a firing squad, his unsympathetic lawyer told him, handing over the judge's formal proclamation. Niori, having admitted to several wrongdoings, had not stood trial but had been sentenced to a hard labor term of 25 years.

Although Mitsuo snubbed the thief himself, he was amazed at the severity of the punishment. Therefore, what was Mitsuo to expect for his own acknowledgment of guilt? He would be executed, certainly, and all his warrior's skills would come to nothing.

Niori's thump to the failing tube had restored its vibrancy. The news tonight was of the war abroad. Mitsuo didn't quite understand whether or not Japan was in alliance with the Germans, but was aware that the two countries held many enemies in common nevertheless. The British had sunk the French fleet in North Africa! How Mitsuo longed to spot that on his maps! Having demanded the surrender of the Gallic vessels or their retirement to a neutral port, the English had not accepted `no' for an answer, but had fired on a former ally, and had scuttled its ships.

Such matters were a puzzle to Mitsuo, and for the most part he wondered only how this would affect Japan's ongoing campaign in the Pacific. Did this mean fewer distractions for the

British in its own war, and therefore more ships free to rally to the defense of the Dutch East Indies and other European protectorates?

Apart from the news of the various fronts–to be worried over without benefit of carefully unfolded charts–Mitsuo had too little to do with his time. He stood on his head and performed energetic exercises to keep himself in top condition–and slept. Full-blown and vivid phantasms came to him at night...

The azure shores of exotic islands appeared below him as he soared. His hand reached for the controls, eyes sweeping the panel of the craft... But no human limb had he, nor was he entombed in a manmade machine. Mitsuo, if that's who he remained, flew, rolled over, turned under power of his own feathered wingspan. He did not require a metal carriage to travel the skies. He, like a hawk, a gull, a broad-spanned, grey-membered sea bird drew narrowing circles in the clouds, seeking a perch, and finally landing on a coral reef bleached by the sun. Facing the deep-rolling Pacific curls, he watched and waited for his prey. The waves lapped against his roost, approaching, departing, with well-ordered irregularity. "I have my duty," Mitsuo, son of Daedalus, said to himself.

...Mitsuo who, as a child of farmers, had not been taught the manners of his betters, had, while a teen, trained himself to sleep as a samurai, flat on his back with a brick as his pillow. The hard pallet in his cell was welcome to him and, on waking, his eyes shot open to a scrim above his head of battleship grey. *Grey*–his mind wandered over some faint connection to that word and specters from his sleep arose. In his unconsciousness, he had escaped the frame of a man. He had transformed into the oldest prototype of the pilot-predator. Concealed within Mitsuo's flesh there lived a falcon. He was destined by the gods to glide, to hover, to ruthlessly annihilate all those who opposed his flight.

Mitsuo trusted that he understood the significance of the pictures which had come to him. He was none other than the raptor, meant to take to the air, intended as a prince of the very stratosphere.

When Nakajima came again, Mitsuo refused to sign the documents. "I can't admit to something I haven't done," the boy maintained.

Nakajima turned his head from the peasant/pilot in disdain.

Still, as the days followed, Mitsuo came to regret his decision more than just once. Simply because he had not made his case easy for the prosecution, didn't mean that his expectation of freedom and a return to the Fliers School would be fulfilled. His mother could not afford a lawyer for him. And who then would defend him? Any protestations of innocence were a mere formality, explained Niori. An accusation was as good as a conviction in the military on a criminal charge. Even Niori was entirely convinced of his cellmate's guilt.

The two talked rarely enough, each man engrossed in thinking his own thoughts–Mitsuo's bleak and Niori's scheming. Battles spoken thrillingly of by the wireless reporters stood as a background to their personal wars.

Germany sank British merchant ships in the Atlantic, while Japan's own troops had subdued all but the entirety of the Philippines. The British issued a foolish and craven warning to Japan to keep out of its own (plundered) colonies.

Not long after, Niori Hiroyoshi was taken away–and with him his radio.

One week following, Nakajima came to Mitsuo yet again, but not to request his signature.

"Miss Ota has tried to kill herself," the prosecutor informed him sternly.

Mitsuo blenched. "Miss Ota is not dead?" he cried out, distressed.

Nakajima observed Mitsuo sharply. "No. The girl isn't dead, but she has lost the child. Just as well I suppose, if anything matters to a scoundrel like you."

Mitsuo tried to digest this new, unwelcome fact, and to

understand the implications of Akiko-san's suicide attempt. It had come, of course, after he had declined to confess. No doubt his refusal had meant further mortification for the girl.

He covered his eyes with both of his palms, then wiped them back across his forehead. "All right. I will sign the confession," he said. "Give it to me."

Nakajima stood, in apparent annoyance. Neither not signing nor agreeing to sign were pleasing to the man. "I'll have the papers typed up again. Then I'll be back. First, I'll inform Vice Admiral Ota personally."

But Nakajima seemed to have forgotten Mitsuo, who waited in vain to fulfill his final function. He paced his cell on his hands and then on his feet. If only he could hear the war news–at least that would distract his mind for a while. He was a boy of the greatest discipline but there were moments in this place where he actually felt that he might go mad. Let him sign! Let them shoot him!

Three days later, a visitor was announced and Mitsuo, who had not washed in a disgracefully long period of time, slicked back his hair and as best he could, tidied himself.

His visitor was not the prosecutor, however.

Miss Ota herself sat in the chair in which his heartbroken mother had not long before rested. Mitsuo sank into the seat opposite. "Miss Ota, oh, do not distress yourself. You ought not have come here. This is a filthy and horrible place. Please let me call the guard to have you escorted home."

In fact, the girl did look distraught–thin and out of sorts–and her lip trembled as she sat, eyes down, scrutinizing the table, and that alone.

"I have done you a terrible harm," her voice cracked out. "I lied. Of course I lied. You know that already. I have done wrong and I beg your pardon. No, stop. I know that you cannot forgive me. I can't ask you that. But I beg you to hear my apology anyway."

"Miss Ota, Miss Ota, never think of that. I only wish that you hadn't tried to kill yourself. Please promise me that you will not do anything of the sort again." Mitsuo nearly swooned with rapture at his own eloquence and at hers. This was a scene such as he might have dreamed. Perhaps he had. Was he awake by any stretch of the imagination? He had, all his life, yearned to lift himself out of a peasant's cloak and to take a stance that befitted someone born above his own low station. What a remarkable experience! The boy's soul shined in exultation.

"Three days ago when the prosecutor came and told us you were ready to confess, I wrote my father a letter and told him the truth. The baby was Kinsuke's. And now I've killed it, rather than myself." Tears gushed out of the young girl's eyes. "How could I have? I loved him. Foolishly, it's true, but I did."

Mitsuo was somewhat taken aback by the girl's words. Of course, there had to have been another man in this scenario, but Kawabata! A love affair–not a rape! He choked. "Kawabata, that devil. It's good he's dead or I would have to kill him now myself."

The awful scandal could hardly be undone. Released from military prison, Mitsuo was not returned to Tsuchiura, but was granted a *de facto* graduation with his class. He was flown out to the Philippines, to a formerly American airfield where no classmates had been posted.

The accusation and his stay in jail were a nightmare that had passed, leaving Mitsuo numb and disoriented. He climbed into the cockpit of the plane assigned him and tried to refamiliarize himself with the controls.

His fellow pilots broke out a bottle of local wine to welcome him. Mitsuo, who never touched a drop, now drank.

They toasted Japan's domination of half the world. "Once Pearl Harbor fell and the American battleships with it, we had the Philippines directly in our pocket," boasted Koiso, a pilot from Nagasaki.

"Soon the British will concede and run."

"The Pacific is ours as it rightly should be," agreed another of the fliers.

Mitsuo felt nothing at all to hear such intoxicating words. His blood ran neither warm nor cold. He was like a wild boar in the woods who had been struck deeply by a wounding arrow, but had not been killed.

Mitsuo's mind clutched at the old beliefs in the warrior's role, but his heart had been immured in a stronger dungeon of its own and could not respond.

In the morning, they made a bombing run on Dutch New Guinea.

Whom Slaughter Spared

After breakfast, Hiroaka always seated himself by the aviary, which was where he was now–reading the morning newspaper and occasionally clucking indigently to himself. He not only had difficulty believing much of the news the papers reported, but that which he did concede to be true often made his blood boil.

Japan had begun a series of offensives against British territories in the Pacific. Until this had occurred, so long as Japan had refrained from definitively crossing that breach, England had been able to "overlook" other Japanese "initiatives." And Hiroaka had been able to tell himself that maybe he could still consider his country a civilized one. Japan had signed an agreement with the United States, after all, and no irrevocable move had been made against Britain.

But Hiroaka's momentary trance had been broken with simultaneous raids on the Solomon Islands–from Guadalcanal, to Rabaul on New Britain; and on Papua and Northeast New Guinea–both administered by Australia, which was, after all, a member of the Commonwealth.

Hiroaka threw the paper down and sat absorbed in the sounds of the parakeets. Their carol was the only thing that could relax him nowadays.

It was unbelievable that Hiroaka had asked the women to go out and buy songbirds, with a war on! his mother, Fusako-san, had told him. Unimaginable, and odder still, was that she had been able to find some at a small shop in the nearby village. Of course, never mind that their shrill twittering got on her nerves; forget about that. Anything to please her child, after whatever appalling hardships he had endured.

Despite the brittle manner in which his mother delivered her set little speech, Hiroaka took her words completely at face value. He was the son, the only adult male left inside their country refuge. They all well understood that he was to be catered to. Completely aside from the circumstances through which the young Baron had lately passed–and the multiple possible deaths he had avoided–the respectful response given him as head of the household was a sun and moon over which no question mark hung.

His mother had handed the small bamboo cage to Hansuko to empty into the larger one. Hansuko was the one maid left to them. As they were near enough to Tokyo, all of the local women had been pressed into service in the factories. And most of the men had gone off to war. It was a wonder that the family was able to get along at all. And where the money was coming from, Hiroaka had no idea!

Tanizaki, his father's steward, was absent, too, was probably part of that mad rifle-bearing mob of automatons hurling themselves against Hiroaka's former schoolmates on New Britain or New Ireland. Hiroaka hated reading about the assaults, shuddered at imagining his roommate Philip, the next Lord Kensington, urging a troop of Cockney Brits with accents so thick you would think that they were speaking Gaelic to shoot none other than the people Hiroaka had spent even more of his life amongst. Body and soul, he was Japanese!

What sense would it make if Philip's bullet struck and felled Tanizaki? Or the other way around? Such thoughts had disheartened Hiroaka since long before the first round had been fired in the South Pacific, but were so much more vivid for him today.

That was why he had done what he had, why he had spied on his country and had delivered secrets to his school friends at the Embassy. If only the British had been able to stop the war at that point!

As Hansuko could only be in one place at a time, and because the mistresses of the household were... somewhere... doing something... no one was left to usher in Hiroaka's visitor, a captain of the Imperial Navy, who popped out into the garden, badly startling Hiroaka. Hiroaka's immediate impulse was to run and hide behind the largish ginkgo at the end of the path. He restrained himself. That would neither be dignified, nor would it work. Hiroaka cast a grim eye upon the stranger, a middle-aged man of distinguished bearing whom Hiroaka didn't recognize.

"Lieutenant Shimazo, I presume?"

"Baron Shimazo," Hiroaka sternly corrected.

The man seated himself next to Hiroaka without asking or being granted permission. "You haven't resigned your commission, I don't believe," he began in a measured tone.

Hiroaka regarded him blankly, as if not following the conversation.

"I'm Captain Suzuki, sent by Admiral Nishizawa to inquire after your welfare, Lieutenant."

Hiroaka stared into his father's English garden, which had become quite overgrown of late, and tried to focus on the socializing noises of the birds. "I'm well, thank you, Captain," he said softly and slowly. "But I wish that I could offer you some tea. How shameful that I cannot do so." Not that Hiroaka actually cared a whit about being hospitable. All he wanted was for this repellent Captain Suzuki to pick himself up and leave.

"We have all had to make sacrifices for the war effort," answered the Captain. "I myself lost an arm two years ago in China. If I had not, I can assure you I would be dropping bombs on Port Moresby in Papua today."

Hiroaka turned and gazed directly at the man, first verifying the loss of the arm–the sleeve, indeed, was an empty one–and then observing the expression on the older man's face, which showed a seriousness that Hiroaka was used to seeing his own father display. Hiroaka flinched inwardly. "Send my best wishes to the Admiral, Captain. Tell him he is welcome to come and see me any time. I will be sure to have some tea for him." This last comment *was* intended as an insult to the Captain, although in times such as these, Hiroaka was unsure who held the real status in society–the Baron or the naval officer.

That issue was about to be debated. "Since you seem fit, Lieutenant, Admiral Nishizawa has authorized me to require you to report to his command, the Eighth Battery in Tokyo."

A bolt of emotional electricity resonated through Hiroaka's frame. He contained himself in a sly attempt to appear not at all moved by the Captain's message.

"I won't be able to do that, Captain." His mouth had gone dry and it was a wonder he had the phlegm even to utter those fateful words. Although Hiroaka had been brought up to himself command, he had also been reared to respect the authority of those above him. In some sense, he had to recognize Suzuki as his superior.

Indeed, a flush of rage flashed across the officer's face and for a moment Hiroaka wondered if he was going to be responsible for the man's stroke or heart attack. The extreme reaction for some reason calmed him, and he took a breath and smiled slightly.

"Why would that be, Lieutenant?" inquired the naval officer coldly.

"I have a great many responsibilities here at home–as you see."

A sneer appeared on the Captain's face–or was Hiroaka imagining things? "The Admiral did not intend for you to leave Tokyo, you understand. And I'm certain a promotion is in store. He wants you there as one of his staff. Of course you would be able to return here from time to time."

"I will certainly consider the Admiral's kind offer." In the seven months Hiroaka had been at home since his release from the naval hospital, he had not once left his family estate. He had no intention of doing so now.

Neither Hiroaka's mother nor his wife Miako could go down to the village for him again this week. That truly was evident, even to someone as oblivious as he. His birds appeared to have a cold or to be otherwise flagging, and Hiroaka wanted some medicine for them. He walked to the gate repeatedly. If he could catch a schoolboy bicycling by or some housewife with a basket, perhaps he could send that individual to the shop where his mother had bought the parakeets.

Finally, with a great sense of unease, Hiroaka undertook the journey on his own. The distance to the village wasn't great and he could use the exercise. Still, not having been out in public for quite a while, and having taken a considerable dislike to noise of any kind, made the trip a difficult one for him.

An automobile stopped and a well-dressed couple courteously offered Hiroaka a ride, but he refused. He was afraid that he would go mad cooped up with them for even a minute or two.

He was aware of the fact that he had become quite odd. Entering the mundane world again was not what he had imagined it would be when he had been marooned on a small coral reef. He had pictured then all the day-to-day wonderful things he would do, but had found upon arriving home that people darted here and there in unpredictable ways, and their conversations were hard to follow. The sounds alone were terrifying. Especially that! Hiroaka worried that if there was too much happening all at once, he would fall to the ground panting and be unable to move. He was certain that something of the sort was bound to occur and could not resign himself to the resultant humiliation.

The only noises that seemed not to bother him were the speeches the birds made to one another and to him, and the conversation of his son Satoshi. His son's voice was like the rush of the sea to the shore, a natural vibration that held no danger.

Arriving at the small settlement here in Shiroi, Hiroaka walked gingerly by the few stores, peering timidly into each. He indicated a bow to all the passersby (no young people among them—all the young people had disappeared), many of whom, of course, he had known all of his life. They restrained any sign of curiosity at the sight of him, and inclined their whole torso deeply to attest to their respect.

No doubt they thought Hiroaka's subdued response a haughty one, but his heart was, instead, fluttering like the wings of a sparrow trapped in a wicker enclosure.

Ah, here was the shop, with sticky rice balls on a tray, fabric in rolls, and, at the back, a row of hanging cages with canaries and other songbirds. Hiroaka entered and made his way down the narrow aisle to admire the bright eyes and exquisitely carved bills. Once his own pair had recovered, he might add some of these beauties to his flock. His grandfather's aviary was spacious and he was sure his mother still had some cash tucked away. Of any details of the estate, however, he was essentially unsure...

An elderly shopkeeper came out from behind a flapping textile curtain and bowed to Hiroaka twice in rapid succession.

"Uh, the birds you sold my mother are sick."

The old man was immediately solicitous.

"Have you a medicine for them?"

The tradesman rummaged through a drawer with some concentration, eventually coming up with a small vial. A drop in their drinking water each day would do, he said.

Hiroaka inquired as to the cost of a pair of pale yellow canaries and indicated that he might be interested in buying them at a later time. He paid for the medicine, then left.

Filled with satisfaction at having done so well on his maiden foray, Hiroaka began the ramble home. About one-third of the way into the trip, he pulled out a sticky rice ball and took a bite. *He was savagely hungry, but he would save the rest for later. He would eat the rice a few grains at a time.*

Despite the warmth of the sun, Hiroaka felt quite suddenly chilled. Where had the rice ball come from, anyway? How had he known the thing was in his sleeve? He stopped walking and his stomach seized up. He tucked the rice ball back into his garment and turned about, pondering.

He could see himself, in his mind's eye, reaching toward the tray of food. Was he, the new Baron Shimazo, a common thief? Had he ever, in his life done such a thing? What had possessed him? *The hand extended itself; the eyes cast a glance toward the storekeeper to make sure the fingers went unnoticed; the thoughts tumbled out, `Here's a bit of rice. I must have it!'*

Hiroaka's jaw set as he marched the distance back to the store.

This time his head sank deeper as he bowed. "I've made a ridiculous error. Please excuse my incredible stupidity. My focus was elsewhere..."

He offered more than enough in coins for what he had taken.

"Oh yes," agreed the shopkeeper without annoyance. "I thought you had forgotten. Your mind, I believe, was on the birds."

"Perhaps you will come and visit me soon," answered Hiroaka, inspired. "I would like your opinion as to the health of my parakeets. Then, too, you must have considerable knowledge about their care. I've only lately come to take an interest in them."

"We heard that you had gone to sea," said the elder. "And that you had then returned home unwell. We prayed for your recovery."

"How kind you've been. I was ill for some time, you understand. I'm grateful to be home..."

He forgot about his fear of dropping to the floor in total confusion and became obsessed with the concern that he would steal again. And what if he should even be caught? At that idea, he would go almost blind with dread!

Perhaps he ought to kill himself. He was a samurai. This was no life for a man such as he.

If he stayed here, never left the estate, there would be no jeopardy.

A polite, but commanding letter arrived from Admiral Nishizawa, requesting Hiroaka to attend him in Tokyo on the Monday next.

There was nothing for it but to kill himself.

He had even forgotten where he had laid his swords, but his father's weapons were in his study. The Baron had collected many fine old blades over the years, but those Shimazo chose to call his own had first been Hiroaka's grandfather's. Hiroaka looked in on them now, then ran his fingers over everything in his father's room. The air was motionless in here, the furniture Western and looming. Still, a second desk closer to the sliding screen, which opened onto a garden of sand and rock, had permitted the Baron (the *real* Baron, Hiroaka's father) to sit on the tatami and work.

Hiroaka took his father's seat on the matting. His knees were not so flexible now, after everything... He looked out. When had the garden last been swept? There were too many random markings there, the passage of too long a time, and too many fretful feet.

Satoshi ran into this playground and began to shoot his wooden gun, bang, bang. Hiroaka supposed the boy was killing men from Shropshire and Manchester, Oxford and London. The child ought to have a wooden sword instead and practice the traditional arts. What kind of father was he to neglect such things?

Miako called to the child to pipe down, warning him that he would disturb his father's nerves. Ahh, so that was how the household saw him nowadays. Like Rochester's poor mad wife in the attic in *Jane Eyre*. They must be glad that he wasn't out-and-out raving. Or violent.

Hiroaka heard his mother calling for him in frustration. He jumped up, somehow not wanting to be caught in his father's room, but the door pushed open before he could exit. He sat lamely at the desk of British oak as his mother escorted in a guest.

This one at least didn't have on a uniform—just a well-cut Western business suit. And Hiroaka surely would not pick the man's pockets. What harm could come of this interview? Nevertheless, he felt apprehension.

Hiroaka rose and bowed limply, then resumed his seat.

As Hiroaka's mother slid shut the door, the guest, in turn, offered a judicious bow.

"Please sit," Hiroaka invited in a half-hearted fashion. He studied the visitor, hesitantly. The cloth their guest wore was European and richly woven. At length, Hiroaka had to acknowledge that the man might be his social equal. "It's thoughtful of you to have come all this way."

"I wanted to offer my condolences, you see. Then I heard that you weren't well, so I waited. As I'm sure you know, I had spent some time with your father in Germany. He and I often exchanged views there. I could not believe that he was killed–or for what reason."

Hiroaka cocked his eyebrows inquiringly. Who was this man?

"Forgive me. I thought that you remembered, but I see that you do not. You were quite young when we met at the Summer Palace. I'm Count Asano." The Count focused sympathetic eyes on Hiroaka. "I was resident in Germany as Ambassador when your father was there. I knew that he could not have betrayed our country as those who assassinated him had claimed. He was loyal, more than faithful, and a stalwart of the Emperor. He was a fine man, a talented diplomat and politician."

"A traitor? Is that what they said?" Hiroaka was only dimly aware of the specifics of his father's death. He had been so absorbed in his own affairs... Perhaps he had not wanted to know the facts. He was sorry to hear of them now.

"Strategies for the Japanese advance found their way into British hands. You didn't know? A few, a radical few, blamed the Baron. Ishiwara and the others were in opposition to your father's overall intentions, of course–the drive south rather than north, for one particular."

Hiroaka's father had been the target of assassins! According to the tales spun when Hiroaka was a child, he ought to leap up, sword in hand, and take after the men who had butchered his parent. Ahh, such an action had never been in him, and even less so now, when he was greatly fatigued.

Suddenly, Hiroaka pictured Joji's face before him. Hiroaka's father was forgotten in the memory of Joji's voice and the story of the Count's lost son.

Miako entered with a tray, laying out the hot water and tea for Hiroaka, then withdrawing. The two men fell into a silence while Hiroaka measured the finely ground powder and whisked the tea.

"Very nice," remarked the Count appreciatively as he sipped. "One gets nothing like this abroad, of course."

In fact, the women provided nothing quite so good for Hiroaka alone. "Yes," Hiroaka agreed. "The only thing I missed at Oxford was a decent green tea." He smiled more broadly than he had in a long while. "The English pride themselves so on their tea, but they have nothing like this, I don't believe."

"No, not even the English, although I have a taste for a Twinings suchong once in a while," mused the Count.

The two men drank their beverage companionably. Hiroaka felt warmed by the thought of being for a change with someone of his own kind.

"What are you doing now that you have left the Navy?" inquired the Count.

That was a brutal reminder of the Admiral's summons. Hiroaka reached at random for an answer. "I was considering organizing my father's papers. Surely history will wish to see a Prime Minister's notes."

"Ah, you have a sense of the political, very much like your father did."

"I suppose that the governance of nations matters a great deal to me. Decisions made by politicians have a very material impact on the lives of those who follow them."

"I'm not sure just what you mean," replied the Count, contemplating the young Baron's words. "Surely it must be the other way around. Because men dedicate themselves to those who rule, great deeds may thus be carried out. That is what I saw in Germany, I must admit–something of the sort that we so strive for and admire here."

"Certainly, that's what I intended to say," Hiroaka concurred. Of course, it was not.

He was too far from the aviary to hear his birds, yet nonetheless he opened his ears for their crooning. They were such harmless little beings–sheerly fluttering joy on the wing, brother creatures. Happily, the parakeets had overcome their doldrums and Hiroaka hoped to soon add to his brood.

"I am posted to Tokyo as advisor to the Prime Minister," the Count continued. "I could use a young, educated man like you to help me formulate proposals for General Tojo to put forth. If you are half the thinker your father was, I would be pleased to take you on. You could remain home to work on your father's memoirs and come into Tokyo as the need arises. We are on the verge of striking at the Australian mainland, you understand, but are unsure of the timing. The Australian forces are surprisingly weak, according to the aerial reconnaissance reports."

Hiroaka shuddered inwardly. Such a step against Australia was the one that he most feared. Could they be mad enough in Tokyo to take on that vast continent? How he would hate to have a hand in it! Yet he had a far deeper aversion to serving the Admiralty. "I accept," Hiroaka agreed, smothering his trepidation. "I will begin considering the matter." Was the conquest of Australia the ultimate goal for which his father had planned?

Mr. Nakajima arrived with his canaries, proffering them as a welcome-home present for the young Baron. Great joy washed over Hiroaka's face as the men hung the new cage inside the larger one, allowing the birds to get acquainted before they mixed.

Hiroaka gave Mr. Nakajima tea, though nothing so fine as that served the Count the day before. Satoshi came out and played busily at the men's feet.

"How lucky you are to have a son," commented Mr. Nakajima.

"One of my few pleasures in life," agreed Hiroaka. "Along with the birds. To be candid, I am no longer comfortable in the society of men. I find them harsh and their behavior erratic. I grew unused to them where I was for a time, and now I find them virtually unacceptable–potentially violent, with hidden

93

motives of the darkest sort."

"All that is true," acknowledged the old merchant, gravely nodding. "But a man's existence cannot be centered on avoidance. The more that you back away from difficult encounters, the greater the number of situations that will bother you. There is no possibility, nor need, either, for any of us to be entirely at our ease in this life."

Hiroaka pushed that thought around. "You can't imagine what I go through... A noise, for instance, will agitate me so, for hours... You mustn't think that I was like this before the war. No, not at all. I was content... Until I went to sea." The marvel was that Hiroaka trusted the shopkeeper enough to tell him his troubles.

Mr. Nakajima swallowed some of the everyday tea and his face lit up with genuine enjoyment. "Man is not the master here, and we do not know ourselves at all."

"Mysticism, I suppose?" Hiroaka scoffed at the old man's words. The West looked down on the Japanese for just such mumbo jumbo.

Mr. Nakajima's burnished eyes pierced Hiroaka's. "Withdrawal from the world is a form of living death. Is that mysticism or practicality?"

Hiroaka shook his head, but he had already ceased to pay attention.

Hiroaka had been thinking of Joji ever since the Count's appearance at his home. As he wrote to the Admiral explaining that he was engaged by the Count and would be unable to serve the Navy directly, Hiroaka's thoughts returned again and again to the kidnapped boy. The child Mitsuo was a flyer for the Navy. Surely Hiroaka would be able to track him down.

At the conclusion of his formal refusal to Admiral Nishizawa, Hiroaka penned a request that he might be told the whereabouts of Sakano's son. He wanted to see the boy, to know how the noble offspring had turned out under Joji's tutelage. He wished—if it was not too late, if the boy were not absolutely spoiled–to discover what could be done to right a grave wrong.

The Admiral would think this a strange letter, indeed. And so it was, but Hiroaka did not mind at all. He would do as he desired. His great-grandfather had ruled an entire province, a fiefdom. Lord Shimazo had commanded thousands of men, and his word had been law. Surely Hiroaka, his descendent, could rule himself.

Or was that impossible? Perhaps the old man, Mr. Nakajima, had known better than Hiroaka in this regard.

On Hiroaka's first trip into the city, in an automobile sent by the Count, the young Baron sat and trembled and tried to quell a bout of nausea. He was certainly not in command of his mind or his limbs. He was ill, pitifully unwell, ruined for life.

Once at the Prime Minister's offices, Hiroaka recovered somewhat and enjoyed meeting with men whom he had known at school, men of breeding, like himself. There were no Jojis here.

Then again, he continued to hold Joji as a beloved confidant hidden inside himself, someone who had been especially close, with whom he had shared the depths of despair and the longing for survival.

Also within his subterranean being flew verdant companions with sharp beaks. Mad? Of course he was. Hopelessly so.

Home again was a tremendous relief. Almost.

"Shall you get a stipend from the government?" questioned his mother.

"I've forgotten to ask. Is that usual?"

"Dear boy, we have investments, of course, but the estate is no longer making any profit. There are no men to harvest or to sow."

"I see." He frowned. He had hardly paused to think of the matter at all.

Hiroaka traveled again to Tokyo several times. The trip was an easy one, really, from the car to the Ministry, lunch with the Count, intellectual conversation, then back to the estate. He enjoyed the bright wit of equals, but their philosophies rankled. War was nothing to these men. The prospect of the death of many–for a glorious cause, after all–did not weigh on them.

Hiroaka urged caution in expanding the conflict to the Australian mainland. Having ventured into British territory, and being on the verge of taking Papua and the rest, however, the Japanese higher echelons were nonchalant about widening their efforts.

There was word of a British flotilla forming, and rumors that the United States, despite its pact with the Nippon Empire, would enter the fray. Hiroaka reminded his fellow advisors of this. No–these were men who had gotten the scent of blood and the vein was not their own. What did they worship? The Emperor himself now preached restraint. Did anyone hear him?

Hiroaka received a letter from Captain Suzuki congratulating him first of all on his appointment to the Prime Minister's office, and then conveying current information on Pilot Sakano, who had been injured in the Solomon Islands and was now recuperating at a hospital in Tokyo.

Hiroaka's heart leaped with gladness at the thrilling news. What he wished for, more than anything it seemed, was to meet Mitsuo, as if the boy were his own brother.

Since the Ministry's car was more or less available to him on his trips to meet with Count Asano, Hiroaka mustered all the courage that had been cultivated in him since childhood to direct the driver to a different route. The uproar in the vicinity of the hospital was unnerving–sirens, first of all, and then a ferocious mastiff chasing them through the streets. How fond of dogs Hiroaka used to be! No longer. Yet the young Baron recalled Mr. Nakajima's words of warning about evading unpleasantness.

Outside the naval hospital there was a small shop and Hiroaka hesitated. He wanted to bring the wounded boy some token, some small treat. The impulse to a kindly gesture was so strong that it carried his feet into the store, where he bought a nearly ripe melon for the patient.

Asking for Sakano at the reception area, Hiroaka was

directed to an immense ward of injured and ill sailors and flyers. He recoiled inwardly. He had never before seen such a vision of Hell, even during his own hospital stay. At a loss as to how to find Mitsuo, Hiroaka asked the nurses again and again. This was the Underworld and Hiroaka was therefore himself a ghost.

Bandages on arms, on legs...heads swaddled, eyes patched...and men whose features were virtually burned off. What had Mitsuo's fate in battle been?

A final young woman in white pointed Hiroaka to a bed and he approached with great misgiving. A young man's lively eyes examined Hiroaka's face as he came nearer, irresolutely lowered his head, then looked again. What was the boy's injury? "Sakano Mitsuo?" he asked.

"I'm Sakano, yes."

Hiroaka bowed and tried to smile, inspected the flier, searching for traces of the Asano lineage. "I was a close friend of your father Joji," Hiroaka declared. "He took care of me before he died."

Hiroaka set himself on a stool beside the bed and placed the melon he had brought onto a bedside table. Glancing back, he saw that young Mitsuo was in tears.

"So he is dead then?" questioned the boy, sitting up, sobbing.

Mitsuo was crying for his father–a low sort of person whom Hiroaka had once thought of as absolute vermin. Yet Mitsuo grieved for him while Hiroaka had not once mourned his own father, a fine and cultured man of stature who had showered love on Hiroaka.

Seeing Mitsuo's free-flowing tears, which were accompanied by unstiffled sobs, Hiroaka, too, began at last to weep without restraint. He felt the truth like a knife point in his heart. He had adored and respected his father, and had been the cause of the old Baron's death.

Mitsuo and Hiroaka sat and sorrowed for their losses until Hiroaka, gasping in a breath, cut off his lamentation. He wiped the round drops from his face and smiled at the other man.

"What is your wound?" he questioned quietly.

Mitsuo demonstrated a bandaged hand. "I've lost three fingers. I'm not much good for a pilot anymore. Don't know how I'll farm with this, either." The young man clenched his jaw fiercely, turning his head toward the nearest bed, where another troubled sailor lay wearily staring into the dismal room.

"Never mind, Mitsuo. I'm determined to return your father's care of me. I'll tutor you, prepare you to go back to school. We'll find a suitable place in life for you."

The boyish face lit with elation, then that brightness dimmed.

"I'm sincere, Mitsuo. I'll do whatever I can for you. I have no other purpose in my life." He wanted to help Mitsuo but not exactly in order to pay Joji back. What plagued him most was that the seaman had died without expiating his extraordinary crime. Hiroaka would take on that burden for Joji; that was the form his compensation would take. And, in some sense, he would also do it for his own father–who had considered matters of rank to be so sacrosanct. In raising Mitsuo to his proper station, Hiroaka would do the old Baron honor.

And additionally he wanted to. He simply wished to do this thing.

Admiral Nishizawa and three of his aides showed up at the meeting with the Prime Minister. The single topic on the agenda was a strategy for subjugating the remaining territories in the South Pacific and surrounding seas.

Asano spoke for the Prime Minister in pointing to the map and declaring, "New Zealand is the natural extension of our realm. Once we have solidified our gains in New Guinea and have completed several airfields in the Solomon Islands, our push further south will be inevitable. If the British fleet arrives, it will do so too late."

A sense of warm gratification at future victory seized hold of the men. They were the leaders of a five-thousand-mile-long Japanese Empire, a growing, spreading, living organism dedicated to their Divine Emperor and their own aspirations.

"We have defeated not only every country we have taken on," pronounced the Prime Minister, "but we have conquered the myth of Caucasian supremacy. We will rule from China to Tasmania, the bottom of the world. The Emperor's flag will fly over one-third the globe."

Hiroaka struggled for the arguments that would turn back this virulent tide. But why? Why did he fight against it so? Had he, too, been cowed by the idea that the West was culturally superior to the East? Was it, in fact, Japan's ordained calling to replace the British in the Asian sphere? He hesitated.

Admiral Nishizawa, a bulky giant, and somewhat stiff in the joints, approached the map. Instead of indicating the natural flow of Japan's troops and bombers toward the south, he used a still-strong finger to sketch the routes the British were already taking from India and South Africa. "Enormous distances? Yes, so it would seem. And our hold over Indonesia gives us command of the Java Trench"–he stabbed at the map–"and the North Australian Basin. The strategic advantage is certainly ours. The British, however, need not circumnavigate the Australian continent, merely crawl up along the coast, thusly." The finger moved relentlessly. "Two or three aircraft carriers and they transport a complete counteroffensive."

"As our bombers fly in from New Guinea," objected Asano.

Hiroaka was dazed. He could smell the sweat of men crowded together in the dark Western-style chamber. His mind darted here and there, seeking an escape from the room before he burst out with words that could not be recalled. Then, suddenly, making a decisive move, he stood before them. "Admiral Nishizawa's cautions were my father's also," he pronounced forcefully.

"He advocated the drive south–not toward Australia, by any means–but in order that our own troops not be spread too thin for ultimate success. We may be able to subdue New Zealand, even Australia, but can we hold them? What native troops will stand with us and which will work against us underground? How many Japanese will it take to retain a land that we have disposed of militarily? These are questions that come not from me alone, but are the voice of my father in the papers that he left behind.

"There was no more loyal Japanese national than my father. He was murdered by traitors–not by supporters–of the realm. His vision was for a powerful Empire greatly outlasting Hitler's projected thousand-year Reich. But to do this means a building step-by-step, decade by decade, century by century, even as what has gone before! Our ancestors forged their domains over epoches. They reached out time and time again, adding to their lands as they went, little by little. If we are too greedy at this one interlude, we will forfeit our future. Of that my father was certain, and I, a devoted son, must say the same."

The meeting terminated not long after, with the Prime Minister protesting that "times have changed," while the others remained swayed by Hiroaka's emotionality, if not his logic.

Drained, the current Baron stepped into the car and the driver headed for the Shimazo estate. Had Hiroaka betrayed his father yet again, or had he memorialized him? He had not even glanced a single time at the old Baron's papers since returning home. Once he had been so fascinated as to what fabrications his father's documents held, yet in the last few months, his indifference had been total.

Hiroaka leaned back in the car and reached into his sleeve. *Yes, the orange was there. He had nearly taken it out during the meeting, had nearly peeled the fruit and broken off a sliver to wet his mouth. The thirst, the thirst had been so terrible on that island. Yet the birds had made him one of their own. He could have stayed there with them for all eternity, pecking away at the newly budding coconuts and drinking the brackish water delivered from time to time by Heaven itself.*

If he was still a man, that remained for the gods to reveal. Where did his future lie? Where? What must he do?

"Let me off in Shiroi," Hiroaka, clearing his throat,

commanded the driver. "There's a shop that sells songbirds. I want to stop there."

Perhaps Mr. Nakajima could explain to Hiroaka how to unravel the terrible tangle he had become.

The Dead Lie Long

Although Miriam had not spoken German out loud in twenty years, today a refrain from a Heine poem kept pushing its way into her thoughts:

The dead stay dead forever
Only the living live
My joyful heart is bounding

But she could not recall the line after that.

The dead never did re-emerge, except in one's memories, or in one's dreams. Miriam's mother and father were still dead. Minoru Shimazo–Baron Shimazo, that was–and the man she had married at the Baron's behest, Isoroku Tanizaki, were dead as well. Long dead. Tanizaki had perished in the first wave of assaults on the beaches of Cape Reinga, the northernmost–and supposedly unprotected–tip of New Zealand.

The year had been 1941; that was when the news had come. Tanizaki was dead, leaving none behind who could sincerely grieve.

The lack of mourners was the saddest fact of all, thought Miriam. She went through the forms–even lit a candle and said kaddish, the prayer for the dead. She had done that for the Baron, too, although she wasn't sure why. Miriam didn't know whether God cared one way or the other about her prayers, or whether the effect on her son of seeing the ritual was for the better or the worse. There was no sense in inculcating him into the ways of his mother's lineage. Being a Jew would do him no good in this country, would only set him further apart. There had been enough of that in Miriam's life.

She woke up to the screaming of the maid Oharu and knew at once that their dwelling was on fire. Nothing is so frightening as a fire in the middle of the night, but a blaze in a Japanese house, all wood, paper, and straw flooring is particularly terrifying. Little Noburu slept right beside Miriam and she picked him up, throwing off his blanket, for fear that the material would too quickly burn if touched by the flames.

Thick, whitish, pouring smoke surrounded them, but she grabbed Tanizaki's sword which she kept nearby, and thrust it in front of her, using it as a blind man would use a cane to find his way. Pieces of pottery shattered around them, then she smashed her way through the paper screening to the outside.

What must she do now? Oharu's shriek still filled the air but Noburu was bawling loudly as well. After a long, worried moment, Miriam set the baby down in the garden and ran toward where she believed Oharu's room to be.

What if Noburu began to fuss, to toddle toward the pond? What if he drowned during her attempted rescue of the maid?

Kerosene, that was what she smelled. Or gasoline. Certainly they had no volatile materials of that type in their house.

Using the still-sheathed sword as a poker, Miriam dashed into the disintegrating structure. "Oharu," she called, again and again, but by now the woman's howling had died down and Miriam still couldn't find her. She dropped to the floor and crawled through the blistering, flaming house as her lungs filled with smoke and ash. After a short while, she turned back.

That was all that she could venture. With a coughing fit tearing at her lungs, Miriam retreated. She managed to find her way into the garden where Noburu had tottered onto his feet and was laughing at his own astonishing pluck.

There was nothing Miriam could do but watch the house burn, and Oharu with it.

Careful to observe that no wind swept the sparks toward any of her neighbors' property–not likely as the closest was a mile or so away–Miriam then trekked up to the big house with the baby in her arms.

The next day, the women searched and found the maid's blackened body among the charred ruins. Miriam sobbed for Oharu as she had not cried for Isoroku. Might Miriam have entered the house a little more quickly–tried somehow harder to get the girl out?

And if her one-time lover Hiroaka Shimazo was also dead, Miriam really did not know, nor did his wife Miako know either. If Miako had known, Miriam would have quickly found out, because the two women happened to be the best of friends.

A couple of months after Hiroaka had gone off to sea, Miriam had realized that she was pregnant. Naively perhaps, she had told Baron Shimazo. Not only did she not know what else to do, she was convinced that she owed her benefactor that revelation.

The Baron was, by then, as Prime Minister, deeply absorbed in affairs of state. He rarely returned home at night. Some time went by after she had informed him of her circumstance, therefore, without any particular response from him. Miriam considered that Minoru had forgotten about her condition, or that he intended to do nothing in that regard.

Instead, perhaps three weeks later, the Baron called Miriam into his study and announced that he had arranged for her to marry his steward, Isoroku Tanizaki, a man Miriam had seen around the estate, but to whom she had never spoken even a word. She smiled wanly and mentioned that fact.

"That doesn't matter," responded the Baron at once. "Tanizaki is kind and he understands the arrangement very well. He will take good care of you, as he always has my estates. There is money and property in your name, should it ever come to your wanting to leave him. But I doubt very much that such a thing will become necessary." He paused and looked at her for a moment, then continued perusing the papers in which he was engrossed. Miriam waited for him to wave her away, but he did not do so.

Finally, he glanced at her again. "The child is Hiroaka's,

we may suppose."

She said nothing.

"I will have it presumed so," Shimazo informed her emphatically. "At least among those who need to know anything at all. That is, you and I and Tanizaki will conclude it thus."

"Of course," Miriam agreed, understanding him at last. The Baron had made the matter clear in this way because the child might be his own, and he didn't want that question to arise. It was only left for her to puzzle out why, why he might want to deny–between just the two of them–his possible fatherhood of the child.

Minoru would never have wanted Hiroaka to have known the truth if the child were not Hiroaka's, Miriam thought now–20 years later. He had loved Hiroaka so; he wouldn't have wished to see him hurt. Today, that struck her as the only possible explanation for the Baron's words.

At the time, Miriam had believed that Shimazo's primary motive was political. Having a mistress, even in one's own home, was not the scandal in Japan that it would have been in the West (although such news was never welcome to a wife), but having a foreign mistress, a Western mistress at such a xenophobic period might have done Shimazo's reputation a grave harm.

Oh, maybe something of the sort had passed through the Baron's mind, Miriam conceded to herself, but surely what had mattered to him most was Hiroaka. In many ways, he had sacrificed everything for his son, had at the last taken the traitor's punishment that ought to have been meted out to Hiroaka.

"Congratulations on your marriage," Miako had told Miriam in a halting yet charmingly accented, idiomatic English. Miriam was learning Japanese, of course, but not quickly, whereas Miako, so well brought up, could speak quite competent British English.

"Thank you." Miriam blushed. She had really not done right by Miako and wasn't sure if the other woman knew it. Was Miako aware that Miriam had slept with her husband? "I would like to continue to come up to the house and tutor Satoshi."

It had seemed strange to Miriam at first that Hiroaka's wife would even speak to her. But then she had realized that Miako was very simply lonely. There was in reality no one else to whom the young woman might talk; and Miriam herself, aside from the Baron, had not one single friend here either.

Tanizaki proved to be a respectful husband; which was to say that he in no wise approached Miriam on a sexual basis, for which she was grateful. She simply had no interest in the middle-aged functionary whose jowls sagged so low that his neck itself appeared to droop.

But Miriam took it upon herself to be a satisfactory wife in the ways that counted with the Japanese. She ran the household efficiently even as she went along with her pregnancy; in fact, she took matters so precisely in hand that Isoroku-san, himself meticulous in all such details, praised her on occasion in a tone of surprise.

Miriam was German, after all, not only Jewish, but German—for she had been reared as a German first and as a Jew only secondarily. How strange it was then that her country had turned on her family and on her. But Miriam preferred not to think about those things anymore. She had a great deal with which to occupy her mind anyway, especially once Tanizaki, despite his age, was drafted into the Imperial Army.

Miako took Miriam's visits to teach her son as an occasion to invite the Western woman to share some tea. Distant but friendly in the way that Japanese women often could be, Miako nodded at Miriam's womb one day and inquired in quite typically vague Eastern fashion: "A nobleman in the making, perhaps?" That meant in effect that Miako understood the child not to be Tanizaki's. Tanizaki was of a samurai family, of course, but was definitely no more "noble" than that.

Miriam did not wish to rebuff Miako's small gesture of commonality, but was unsure how exactly to answer. "The child will be a Tanizaki, naturally," she replied with care. While the Baron had stipulated that between himself, Miriam, and Isoroku, the child was to be considered the Baron's grandson, Miriam was certain he had not meant for her to acknowledge that to Hiroaka's wife.

Despite all the possible differences between the two, the women grew close. When the Baron was murdered on his way into the Palace for a conference with the Emperor, Miako rushed to inform Miriam, gazing with soft eyes of sympathy, as one would at a woman who had lost her lover. Miriam returned with Miako to the main house to extend condolences to Fusako-san. Minoru's wife received Miriam's solace grimly, gave her tea and rice cakes in a proper fashion, and sent her away. Of course Miriam was grieving for the Baron–as so, too, her heart often ached for Hiroaka, then somewhere in the wide Pacific.

When Miriam began to have contractions, she sent Oharu running to the Shimazo house, and Miako arrived at the Tanizaki cottage before the midwife did.

Miako's calls upon the Tanizakis did not cease with the homecoming of Hiroaka, either, although then Miriam did not walk up to the main house anymore. She avoided any meeting with Hiroaka, but waited, tensely certain, for his approach.

But he did not come to her, and did not come.

As his son–or was it his father's son?–went from crawling to the toddler stage, Miriam wept many times on seeing Hiroaka from afar. But she knew that he was right.

Miako kept Miriam apprised of Hiroaka's comings and goings. Miako was proud of her husband, who had become an advisor to Count Asano–himself an advisor to the Prime Minister–but she was puzzled by the man. She confessed frankly to Miriam that Hiroaka had not slept with her since his release from the naval hospital and, although it was not completely unusual in a marriage, they did not talk at all. Miriam wondered if Hiroaka might be longing for her to come to him, but she could discern no indication.

Then one day, surprisingly, Hiroaka left home again. Miriam assumed that he had returned to active duty at sea, but Miako, too startled by the sudden turn of events to weep, even modestly for appearances sake, disabused Miriam of such a notion.

"He's become religious," she told her friend in candid astonishment, "some kind of a Buddhist." Shinto was unquestionably the preferred religion among the elite, and Miako said the word Buddhist, as if it were completely foreign to her–odd. "He's making a retreat in a monastery. He'll be back before long though, I'm confident."

That had been some 19 years ago and Hiroaka had not been home at all since then. Memories of him for the women were covered over by the kind of spottiness that time inflicts upon the vibrancy of the brain. Hiroaka was not particularly of importance to the two of them anymore, anyway–did not figure into their daily lives. No men really seemed to, except the now-grown children.

"Fusako-san refuses to have you and the child living in the house." Miako had confessed this, her eyes on the ground. Surely both Fusako and Miako believed that Miriam had been the old Baron's mistress.

The fire, it was evident, had been caused by arson and Miriam and Miako were convinced that they knew the ruffians who had set it. According to the elderly policeman investigating the case, a local tough named Tomo and his henchman Michio had been heard in the village talking about the gaijin–the foreigner–and how she didn't belong here. There was a lot of feeling against Westerners in Japan at the time, no doubt a "natural" outgrowth of the country's martial attitude–but no one would have taken up arms against someone like Miriam who had been directly under the Baron's protection. Then again, in normal times, no one would have assassinated Baron Shimazo himself. And in neither outrage had anyone been brought to justice–another reason for Miriam's move out of the district after the house had been destroyed.

She wept many nights thinking of Oharu, a 15-year-old child, and the unfairness of Tomo's going unpunished. Miriam's pretty little home had been turned to debris, and now she and Noburu must live in a smaller, less comfortable setting. Thinking that way made Miriam feel too self-indulgent. Those who were dead no longer had houses at all: her mother and father and perhaps thousands of other Jews in Germany. (It wasn't until long after that period that Miriam learned of the systematic extermination of millions at the death camps; so little news from Europe reached Japan.)

Thankfully, the Baron had provided for Miriam as he had promised, as well as for his own immediate family. And Miriam soon discovered that she had a flair for watching over those investments. She and Miako met regularly, in part, to manage the family holdings.

Miriam puzzled out the financial moves to make, while Miako would carefully write the business letters in her fine hand. Fusako, who in general trusted no one other than herself, unexpectedly allowed the two to take over without making a fuss. Perhaps after Hiroaka had left, Fusako had simply given up on her life.

Miriam was astute about economic patterns. She was able to see the larger picture. The more territory that Japan held, she perceived, the greater the potential markets for certain Japanese goods.

New Zealand had been completely occupied by Nipponese troops, but the struggle continued inside Australia. Men and equipment were poured into the southern front and while Miriam had moralistically decided not to back armaments per se, she had no such compunctions about placing money in a plant that packaged foods for the troops abroad, or investing in the making of Army uniforms. These operations, she decided, after the war could be turned to peacetime use.

The extended family was flourishing. There was income to send the boys to one school or another, and after the signing of an uneasy armistice in 1949, there was money to hire as servants soldiers returning from the front. Miriam and Noburu moved to Tokyo, to a considerably more comfortable home. She and Miako kept in touch, however, and still made joint decisions about their properties. The two went shopping from time to time, or met for lunch, but both women were busy, as women running households often are.

The bulk of their investments, although managed by Miriam, still belonged to the Shimazos. Miriam considered this more than fair, since she had entered this country with only the clothes on her back, at the mercy of the Baron's generosity and tender heart. That she had enough to live on and to support her son was more than sufficient.

The war ended in Europe in 1942, in contrast with the continuation of hostilities in the Pacific. Although England had provided men, planes, and ships to its cousins Down Under, the focus of its aims after Churchill's heart attack and retirement in September 1941 remained in the Atlantic theatre. The United States, apparently burdened by a sense of shame at not entering the war after raids on its own territories, pursued the Lend Lease program until Hitler's ultimate defeat. The manufacture of ships and guns in that country was, nevertheless, limited.

After Germany's collapse under concentrated assaults by England–and due to lack of coherent leadership inside the Reich–the Commonwealth had resources to aid Australia in its ongoing struggle with Japan. A lack of determination, however, and the burden on Britain of European recovery placed constraints on its helpfulness. The enormous Australian continent was essentially cast off. From his sick bed, Churchill wrote condemnations of public policy, but to no avail. So long as the British public felt safe from Hitler's Teutonic hordes, they found it easy to forget about kinsmen so far away as the Aussies were.

Miriam was shocked by England's stance toward its remote associates, but she was relatively indifferent to it all. Western though she was, she now lived in a distant geopolitical sphere and surely was influenced by those around her. So long as the British held Hitler prisoner in his Berchtesgarten fasthold (executing him in 1945, for war crimes), she was content.

Nor was Miriam a bitter woman, by any means. She did not cleave to the past. Yet on occasion she would hear Tomo's name in conjunction with some accomplishment or other and wonder why the man still lived, growing older and rising in business, while Oharu, an innocent, had burned to death in his arson fire. The sound of the maid's screams had never quite left Miriam's ears. Often at night she would awake to the piercing cries and smell the smoke.

Miriam's economic foresight paid off increasingly with the end of hostilities. The occupying troops abroad still had to be supplied. Additionally, New Zealand and Australia, though politically broken down, were quite fertile markets for trade with Japan. Miriam had invested money in a wool-spinning factory and in importing sheep and their many by-products. The companies she backed were blooming.

If Miriam had been a man, she would have been called an industrialist. As a woman, and a non-Japanese, she kept to the background. Most of the proceeds of her unerring instincts, moreover, went to maintain the Shimazos and their estate. Ease was pleasant and monetary security tremendously reassuring, but Miriam Tanizaki did not seek wealth.

Having been tutored in Japanese in order to keep up with Noburu, Miriam could read the newspapers. As always, she was pleased to see the name of a company in which she invested in the financial pages. What a shock it gave her when she saw Tomo mentioned in that very article. That the little arsonist (the murderer!) had been confirmed as chairman of Moritomo Enterprises, sent a chill shooting up Miriam's spine. Reading this brought her back to the days in her sweet little house across from the sprawling Shimazo mansion. As she planted shrubbery by an open field, the Baron waved at her from a seat in his garden. A few months later, she spied Hiroaka in the same spot, absorbed in a book. Thank God Hiroaka had survived his war! Even thoughts of Tanizaki warmed her heart now that he was gone–a good man, a decent man.

And Oharu, that poor soul, who had died in agony–Miriam remembered her quite clearly now, in a way she would not have, had Oharu merely departed to work in a Tokyo factory.

Tomo at the helm of Moritomo was something that Miriam could not, by any means, abide.

Miriam and Miako's hair had begun to turn grey and Fusako had become a harsh, fussy old lady to whom Miako and the maids catered, when next Miriam visited the Shimazo residence.

Miriam offered her friend an accounting of their jointly-held funds. "I'm going to consolidate a large portion of our holdings in Moritomo Enterprises," she added. "It has strong products going through research and development–a new mechanism to replace the vacuum tube for one. I've been reading about it. It's quite revolutionary."

She itemized the rest of their investments and explained to Miako which companies had diversified and which had pursued Big Brother alliances with larger firms.

Miako listened politely, but she hadn't the knack. "Very satisfactory," she acknowledged at last. "We can only thank you for your work on our behalf." She swayed gracefully in her seat, offering Miriam a respectful bow.

Miriam, an honest woman, hesitated. She had not decided whether she would tell Miako everything. "I believe in Moritomo," she went on after a while. "I think we will do admirably well with it. But I'm risking a sizeable portion of our capital here. I feel I owe you an explanation. Tomo Mikawa is the new chairman of Moritomo..."

Miako's eyes grew large. "Oh, how horrible! Then you must remove all our money at once. It's not worth making more if we must invest in a company with Tomo as chairman!"

Miriam smiled. She had truly grown to care for Miako over the years. Miako was a kind and ethical person, without a single shred of malice in her. She could not think as Miriam did.

Revenge was foreign to her nature. "I'm placing the additional money in Moritomo so that I can ruin Tomo," Miriam explained.

"We will direct quite a large portion of the company, you see, a large voting share. I am considering the ways and means. But it's a gamble, you understand. I've been conservative until now and have diversified our investments between the safe and those promising better returns. In addition, in setting out to destroy Tomo, it's possible that there will be a fight for control of the company. The value of our capital may go down."

Miako bowed her head again. "You must do as you see fit, Miriam-san. Even if you were not my friend for so many years, the Baron would have wanted it so. He would not have allowed Tomo to go unpunished. I am from an old samurai family myself, as you well know. There is nothing that I wouldn't chance to honor my own debt to this family and to you."

Throughout the next weeks, Miriam discretely added to her holdings in Moritomo. She took other measures as well. She hired a private investigator to find out as much as possible about Tomo. And she went to visit General Yamashita, a schoolmate of the Baron's—old but still active—who had taken her under his wing and whom she saw from time to time.

After all these years, Miriam encountered Tomo Mikawa at last. Strangely, she had never faced the man in the flesh, although it had often seemed to her as if she had. She had seen his picture in the paper many times, but the impact of his presence was much more powerful than that. The man radiated a sort of authority that accounted for his great success in business. Miriam swallowed to wet a throat that nerves had dried.

General Yamashita, of course, stood in for Miriam. That she attended this meeting at all was an unusual concession—a woman at a business meeting! Unheard of. But she was a Westerner (and she did control the money, after all, an irresistible credential).

"Well, General, it is good to meet with you. I understand you represent a sizeable interest in Moritomo. If there are any questions about my administration, you are free to ask." Tomo was courteous, but he indulged a foolish old man because he must. The chairman was busy! He had many matters to oversee! He glanced at Miriam with some displeasure. He did not approve of her appearance here.

"Do you remember me, Tomo?" Miriam asked, unexpectedly. It had not been her intention to speak.

"I don't know you, Madam. I am sorry. I would have remembered if we had met."

"You set a fire one night in 1941. A maid died. Her name was Oharu."

Tomo recoiled, greatly offended. "You are mistaken, Madam. Set a fire?" He turned to the General. "Is she insane?"

General Yamashita laughed quite pleasantly. He, as the Baron had been, was a sophisticate, not easily influenced by the trickery of others. He had, after all, for much of his life, held a position of power and command.

"I have already spoken to several members of the board and other significant investors in Moritomo," the General replied. "We are demanding your resignation immediately." He nodded across to the president of the company, Moritomo Hiroshi, the son of the founder. "Sakano Mitsuo has been chosen as successor."

Rage flashed through Tomo's eyes and Miriam gripped the arm of her chair. Why should this man frighten her now? She had brought all this about; she was in charge here.

"On what basis am I being dismissed?" Tomo's voice had thickened, but he had not lost his self-control.

"It will be given out that you were incompetent," responded the General without emotion. He was enjoying his role. "We would not like to see you hired by another company at your current level."

Other than his reputation for ruthlessness in business, Tomo's record since 1941 was more spotless than that of many men who had risen as far as he had. Miriam knew this from her investigation. She was also aware that Tomo had two children now at university. What would this do to them?

Tomo was staggered. "Why?' His voice rose rapidly in pitch. "Why?" he wanted to know.

"Oharu," answered Miriam, quietly at first. The tears ran down her cheek. "Oharu," she shrieked.

"I did nothing," Tomo responded. "I did nothing. It's all a madwoman's imagination. And for that, you ruin me!"

Es bleiben tot die toten
Und nur die Lebendige lebt...
My laughing heart is jumping...

Now she remembered the last line of the quatrain. But Heine's words were no longer true for her. "I've youth and joy to give," they read. Miriam had honored the dead and had brought down an evil man, yet she was uneasy. Had she done right? There were so many evil men out there, so many of them, as common as the grasses in the field. About the rest she could do nothing, but she had brought one down.

And Oharu lay dead yet. And Miriam's parents lay long in their graves– another line of Heine's. The number of those she would never see again grew. And she no longer had either youth or joy to give.

She had only what she had presented to the future–her son and his progeny.

That would have to suffice.

(a yearning nation's blueeyed pride)

When Shimazo Hiroaka made his move to Kyoto, he sent Count Asano a note requesting a favor. He asked that the Count assume responsibility for Sakano Mitsuo. It had all along been Hiroaka's design to adopt the young man, and now he begged the Count to take his place. Although not initially Hiroaka's intention, in this way he reunited father and son without revealing to either the other's true identity.

So Sakano Mitsuo took his rightful place within the Count's house, where he was given a proper education befitting his new position in society. He became a man of the world, although he had seen little of anything outside of Japan.

In time, Mitsuo had many opportunities to take a role in varied spheres of Japanese life and showed himself unusually adept at commerce. Import and export were particularly of interest to him and he flew his own plane–outfitted to accommodate his disabled hand–to the far reaches of the Empire in the conduct of trade. Thus it was that Mitsuo ascended the business ladder from rung to rung, and eventually became chairman of an emerging Moritomo Enterprises, and a respected figure in industry.

His hair now steel-gray, Mitsuo's father, Count Asano, maintained a post very near the Imperial Cabinet. Eventually, as he had traveled previously in the West, he was employed as an envoy to re-engage former enemy countries in the interest of economic betterment for Japan.

As the Count explained to his son, Mitsuo, "We hold what they want–their former territories–and they hold what *we* want–their wealth and their markets. We will give a little, and they will too."

"Exactly what will we give?" inquired Mitsuo. He was thinking of how this information might guide future marketing decisions at Moritomo. All his thoughts were on the company and fostering its prosperity.

The Count filled his son's saki cup a second time. "Maintaining a large hostile territory has not been easy for the Emperor."

Mitsuo swallowed the warm rice wine, which went down like the rawest of homemade alcohols. "What lands might be sacrificed and on what terms, precisely?"

"We're willing to make large concessions," admitted the Count. "We want to buy and sell freely in Great Britain and the United States."

Mitsuo frowned. "There's an entire industrial sector in Japan that's dependent on the import of New Zealand and Australian sheep under highly favorable covenants."

The Count accepted this `information' sanguinely. "That's all been taken into account, of course. My sense of it is that the Cabinet is agreeable to ceding back certain more-populous sections of Australia that have been the most difficult to handle." If that was the Count's `sense of it,' then it was abundantly true. "Possibly along with the North Island of New Zealand. We will retain the agrarian portions of each country.

"Our own people have had enough of this seemingly endless guerrilla conflict. And, plainly, in grabbing Australia we had perhaps yanked a tiger by its tail. During the war years, however, our national psychology was admittedly different from that which it is now, in the 1970s. At the time of the fighting, we wanted all of the Pacific, and believed that we could hold it through our superior will alone. Now we are looking West again for peaceful interactions."

Mitsuo smiled in agreement, but he nevertheless held a contrary opinion. Having those territories in their own hands was quite congenial to the businessman in him. "What then?" questioned Mitsuo, pouring in turn a cup for his father.

"Then you accompany me on a trip to Europe and America. What do you think of such a notion? I am the diplomat, and you, the man of industry. Together, we will make a fine team, don't you believe?"

Surprised by the unexpected invitation, Mitsuo looked doubtful. He would not like to abandon the management of his company for long. Nor did he care to leave his wife Akiko, the daughter of Vice Admiral Ota, for more than a day or two. Akiko was a high-strung woman and tended to severe bouts of depression.

Still. he owed the Count everything, was it not so? The totality of what he was today, all that he owned, had come about because of the generous spirit of the nobleman. "I will go on one condition," he replied.

The Count's eyebrows arched.

"We will fly in the *Tsuchiura*. I never trust any pilot but myself at the controls."

Father and son smiled warmly at one another and toasted their forthcoming journey.

England eagerly welcomed the Japanese representatives. The Conservative government hoped to make amends to elements of the public that openly criticized former and present politicians for (a) making too many concessions to the Japanese, and (b) not yielding enough to that Pacific monolith. That is, certain ultra-conservative groups were furious that the leadership had thrown away the British Empire after Churchill had become incapacitated, while a group of Labourites insisted that the past was the past, and that Britain would benefit from opening its doors to now-closed markets in the East.

As Japanese feelers to the British Prime Minister, Edward Heath, had indicated a willingness toward moves that would to some degree satisfy both constituent groups, the Conservatives were anxious to be credited with this political coup. The return of lands to the Commonwealth would help bolster a currently shaky Tory party. The Conservative Cabinet had spent sleepless nights pondering the possibility that Heath was about to lose the confidence of Parliament.

Heath's own deputy, Lord Kensington, was assigned as liaison to the Japanese contingent, and he stuck as close to Count

Asano and Sakano Mitsuo as marmalade to toast. Haggled with to the snapping point during daylight meetings, and wined and dined in palaces and embassies until they hoped never to view another decanter of port upon a mahogany table, the Japanese negotiators strove weariedly to maintain the grueling diplomatic pace.

Certainly the situation seemed ironic, at least to the two chief Asian dealmakers: The Count and his son were assiduously attempting to return something that the other side desperately wanted, in order to obtain a reward that would be greatly to the advantage of both—yet so much toil was required to consummate this act, so many periods of delicate approaches and retreats.

Philip Kensington bundled the Count and Mitsuo into his own car, per protocol, while the rest of the Japanese delegation assorted themselves into the remaining vehicles. Kensington tapped the glass separating passengers from driver, signalling his man to go forward. The Rolls pulled away. Mitsuo swiveled to see what had become of the others. A second Silver Cloud was close behind. He faced front again. The British Lord and the Count were conversing amiably in English, a language in which, once he stepped beyond matters of products and pricing, Mitsuo was inordinately awkward.

Lord Kensington turned toward the Count's son and murmured words the like of which the businessman had heard frequently in the past several days: "the Tate Gallery," "Victoria Station," "Scotland Yard." The Englishman pointed out the window with each utterance and Mitsuo nodded to indicate a studious concentration. Once again, he was being shown the sights. How he already missed the pulsing streets of Tokyo, store signs that he could read, architecture that accommodated itself to the human proportion.

They were headed toward a less populated area for their daily dose of negotiations and had entered upon a speedway alongside an industrial park. Absorbed in his own thoughts of home and the affairs of his company, Mitsuo was shaken into the present by a loud explosion somewhere ahead. Something had ruptured on the road in front of them–the road itself, perhaps–and their driver screeched to a stop, then rammed the car into reverse. Mitsuo glanced out the small back window as again the Rolls halted. The other cars of their party were no longer behind them. Instead, an unfamiliar van had positioned itself so as to block their retreat, and armed men were rapidly alighting from the vehicle.

Mitsuo's body instinctively sought some means of escape, but there was none. His breath came out as a gasp and, checking the lock on the door–a flimsy protection–his sweating hands gripped at the seat leather.

"What the devil?" asked Kensington, leaning forward and rapping repeatedly to catch his driver's attention. The man, a government security agent of some sort, had brought out a revolver as he tried to cut away from the blockade by wheeling the Rolls around.

A single bullet through the windshield stopped his motion with a resounding shattering of glass. The driver slumped against the seat and Mitsuo sprang to open the sliding pane that separated them. Although many years from his own military training, he wanted that gun.

They were surrounded, and the butt of a rifle broke through to them with further splintering sounds. At first, Mitsuo didn't understand the shouted instructions, but in a moment, he found himself being pulled from the car. He looked toward the Count, fearing for the older man's safety, but there was nothing he could do to prevent them from subduing his father as well.

Their captors shot Lord Kensington once in the chest and deserted the diplomat where he lay. The two Japanese were shoved into the back of the lorry, and as it sped away, they could see nothing through well-sealed curtains. Their seizure had taken a matter of moments.

The house in which they were held was large but not well attended to. They were given a chamber pot to serve their sanitary needs and locked in an inner drawing room with little furniture. Where this place was, they could not even begin to guess. The Count knew parts of London, but beyond that, nothing, so that even had they seen where they were going, the location would nevertheless be a mystery to them.

"We're still alive," Mitsuo pointed out in a low voice. "We must be of some value to them." He sought a way to cheer the Count, concerned by the older man's possible lack of resiliency. Mitsuo had been trained as a warrior; he had never ceased to be prepared to die. But the Count's background was so very different from his own that he trembled for him.

The Count, however, appeared loftily undaunted. "Patriots! I suppose they call themselves patriots. Such men always do. They talk among their members, create a world view, and act impulsively, without the diligently gathered intelligence upon which a legitimate government forms well-considered strategy. That is the difference between politics and the actions that these type of men take—and which they claim to be political. You wait and see!"

There was not long to wonder as two florid-faced Englishmen, whom the Japanese had not seen previously, marched in. At least Mitsuo at first believed them to be English, but his eyes met those of one of their abductors and both Mitsuo and the tall, rangy farmer started.

"You!" uttered the Australian after a pause. Both he and Mitsuo stared at one another, equally astonished.

"You bloody wogs," the other man cursed the prisoners, oblivious.

"What's this all about?" demanded the Count coldly.

"I have to talk to you, Jimmy," said the one whom Mitsuo recognized to his fellow conspirator

"We'll talk later." The man called Jimmy pushed the first away. "Right now, we want a letter from the two of you in bloody wog talk, telling them we have you and that they'd better give us what we want." He shoved a pencil and scrap of paper at the Count who looked at these things as if trying to imagine their possible use. The Count wrote his personal notes on handmade writing paper with a gold-tipped fountain pen.

"He's got nothing to lean it on Jimmy, can't you see?"

"And what is it that you want?" asked the Count with curiosity of a rather mild sort, considering the circumstances.

"We want our country back, you bloody bastard." Jimmy was immediately both furious and frustrated.

"I haven't got it," enunciated the Count in his particularly elegant fashion.

Jimmy went to strike Count Asano, but Mitsuo placed his own body before his father's. He put his arm up to fend off the attack.

At the same moment, the first Australian pulled his countrymen away and toward the door.

"Write the note," Jimmy commanded. "I'll be back."

"What is going on here?" the Count asked Mitsuo the moment the two were once again alone.

"I know that man."

"That was obvious. But under what circumstances might you two have met?"

"Just in the course of business, actually," answered Mitsuo. "But there's a little bit more to it than that."

Devising an economic system for a conquered and captive nation was a matter of often violent and sometimes fatal trial and error. By the time Mitsuo had been trading in Australia for a couple of years, there were some ad hoc rules in place. The Australian farmer/ranchers retained and cultivated their own lands and animals. In turn, they were required to sell solely to the Japanese, at whatever prices they could negotiate. Considering the limited boundaries of this type of capitalism, the Nippon businesses were the greater beneficiaries of such dealings.

The tradesmen who regularly visited a few ranches in the hinterlands were accompanied by the armed guards assigned to them, whom they took on in the north before flying into the interior. Further, Japanese soldiers were garrisoned among the ranches for greater control.

Despite all the precautions, there were constant killings in the outback–Japanese officers slaughtered, bodies hidden–and inevitable retaliations like the Swanson farm massacre. In that infamous incident, a clash of cultures had resulted in the burning to death of 30 Aussie whites, including women and children, inside their farmhouse.

On this trip, because a rival firm had recently dropped out of the wool trade, Mitsuo was visiting a couple of unfamiliar ranches looking for new contracts. If the arrangements would save money for him and the firm, he was willing to let a few of his older ranchers go. This was business, after all. What counted, too, was the quality of the wool.

Having just landed on a lone runway near Lake Auld, Mitsuo had settled in at a ranch dubbed *Hyacinth*, "owned" by Avram Nyland and his family. Avram, the cautiously correct, fortyish head of the household, led Mitsuo and Sergeant Watanabe out to the pens, then drove them in his bone-jarring old jeep to some of the grazing fields.

Mitsuo was pleased with the quality of the animals and he was curious about an aspect or two of the operation. When they returned to the main house, they talked outside for a while until the heat of the day became unbearable. Then the three, accompanied by Nyland's sheepdog Lester, walked back into the house and headed for Mitsuo's room. There he had some woven fabric samples he wished to show the rancher.

They found one of Nyland's sheep men, an Abo–Aborigine–methodically pawing through Mitsuo's traveling bag. Watanabe immediately drew forth his sidearm. Was he planning to despatch the man on the spot, spattering human tissue all over the bed, terra cotta flooring, whitewashed walls?

Mitsuo observed Nyland and noted a slight movement on the farmer's part toward the deadly sheep-skinning knife that hung on his belt. Lester let out a subdued growl. Watanabe was the only one of the group heedless of the implications of his threat with the gun. The scenario painted itself graphically for

124

Mitsuo: The Sergeant would kill the Abo; then, quick as a wink, Nyland would skewer Watanabe. Nyland would next turn and kill Mitsuo, as Lester prevented him from defending himself. A tragedy was surely in the making.

Mitsuo stretched out a friendly hand and pushed Watanabe's gun away. "No, no," he told the soldier in Japanese. "I instructed the fellow to fetch me something. Now give me some time alone with Nyland so I can clinch the deal."

Watanabe obligingly tucked away his pistol, still without a thought in his head. He left, moving toward the kitchen, which he considered his own for the duration of their stay.

The Abo had stopped his examination of Mitsuo's goods and stood, still twisted at the waist, gazing expectantly at the Japanese. Avram Nyland remained on guard, his right fist never leaving the vicinity of his waistband.

"What now?" asked Nyland.

Mitsuo waved the Aborigine away. "Now we deal," he answered affirmatively, with a broad smile of the type he believed the Caucasians took as a signal of good will.

He made Nyland an offer considerably under the one he had intended.

"I'll starve at that," Nyland refused.

Mitsuo split the difference with the rancher and reached out and shook the Australian's hand, a foreign gesture he had trained himself to make. The Japanese businessman had concluded a good day's work. The price was a coup! He had, as well, saved the lives of any number of Australians and a few Japanese. He was ashamed of neither accompaniment.

Soon after, Nyland had disappeared from Australia, as Mitsuo explained to Count Asano. Then, too, Mitsuo had moved to Moritomo Enterprises and was engaged in an entirely different industry.

Whether the aforementioned incident and Mitsuo's acquaintance with Nyland would make any difference to the two prisoners today, Mitsuo could not guess. Further, he was unable to predict what *type* of alteration of outcome Nyland's opinion of him might produce. Nyland might well be angry over a business agreement forced on him in a kind of blackmail.

When Nyland returned to meet with his captives, he was alone. Halfway contrite, the Australian seemed to feel an obligation to Mitsuo he could not discharge. He was caught between two uncompromising and opposing forces. "There's nothing I can do to help you," he kept insisting. "It's out of my hands."

"What you've done today will lead to more harm than good for...your country," the Count told him in turn. The Japanese unofficially called Australia `New Japan,' a label the government had nervously discouraged lately in the public press. They now avoided that identification lest the citizens become too attached to the continent and consider it a permanent part of their own nation. The Count sidestepped the name with Nyland, however, for fear of further antagonizing the man.

"We've come to negotiate the independence of a large portion of Australia," Mitsuo told Nyland bluntly after checking with the Count for the word "independence."

Nyland looked at the two disbelievingly. "Oh piss," he exclaimed.

The Count was pleased that the rancher understood the ramification of their abduction. A Japanese treaty with England would be out of the question at this point–impossible. Japan would never again come to this juncture with regard to Nyland's homeland. Year after year, death and devastation would fritter away the resources of that huge territory. This proved his point about the impetuosity of fanatics, Mitsuo could almost hear the Count saying to himself.

Nyland shook his head. "It isn't on the news yet," he muttered. "We've listened to the radio all morning."

The three of them glanced at one another with a single thought. "Two men were killed," Mitsuo said.

"I'd give my own life," Nyland answered. "If Australia could be Australia again." The big man's eyes quickly went bleary.

126

"Not all of Australia," objected the Count. "We're not giving away all of it yet."

"About three-fourths will be returned to the Commonwealth," added Mitsuo.

Nyland breathed in deeply, thinking ponderous thoughts and shaking his head at the impossibility of anything being done to divert the tide he and his fellows had set into motion.

"With a timetable for releasing the other quarter," Mitsuo threw in.

The Count glared at his adopted son. The Japanese government had hardly intended to go that far. Mitsuo shrugged. By that he meant either that they might as well go the whole route with that damned unmanageable country—or that they could go back on their word as soon as they were released.

There was a sound outside the door and Nyland turned at once to leave.

The Count grabbed the man's arm and from the way Nyland accepted the grasp of his hostage and enemy, he was not on the same side as when he had first entered the room.

The Count took a packet of powders out of his pocket. "Here" he said. "One each in a drink will put a man to sleep."

Nyland took what was handed him, but again he shook his head. "I won't." he told them and was out the door, locking it behind.

The two sat heavily in the shabby chairs at the border of the airless, dust-laden room.

"What was it?" asked Mitsuo, referring to the object the Count had given Nyland.

The aristocrat's eyelids fluttered, his only reaction. "Opium powders," the Count answered a moment later, without apology. "I don't function without it. I'll go into convulsions within a few hours. So I hope Mr. Nyland corrects our situation."

"How brave a man, you are," said Mitsuo, in genuine admiration of his companion's sacrifice.

"Some would call me a coward." The Count closed his

eyes. There was not even the tick of a clock to entertain the two; consequently, time stood quite absolutely still.

The Count paced, then leaned over the commode and tried to empty an already empty stomach. He stood back up. "Very unpleasant," he commented in an understatement. Beads of sweat stood out on his forehead and he mopped his face with a silk handkerchief.

Mitsuo only worried that his companion's heart would give out. He poured a glass of water and offered it to the older man.

"I'm all right, really," protested the Count. "I feel a bit better now."

The door burst open and the two recoiled, but it was "only" Nyland.

"Come now," he ordered roughly, beckoning them to follow him.

Mitsuo went to help the Count, who pushed him gently away. In the next room lay quite a sight–the man called Jimmy, with his throat slashed end to end, nearly decapitated.

"He wouldn't take a drink," Nyland explained.

They clambered down an old staircase, this time the Count accepting Mitsuo's assistance.

"I have the van," Nyland said quietly, starting to lead them around to the back.

"The police will be on the alert for it," warned Mitsuo.

"I don't care," retorted Nyland. "I have every intention of being arrested, tried, and hanged."

Mitsuo held his ground. "I wouldn't want to be shot in error," he answered dryly. "At any rate, I'd just as soon they didn't hang you. No publicity about this whole thing, can't you see?" He tried to calculate just where they were. "Are we still in London?"

"Near enough. I'll drive you to a pub at least. You can telephone from there."

The three agreed. They loaded into the lorry–this time

the Japanese up front next to the driver.

"Any of those powders left?" inquired the Count.

"No, sorry. I used them all. I wanted to make sure. I didn't kill anyone with that stuff, did I?"

"Probably not," said the Count, in dismissal. The death of his kidnappers was of no relevance to him. "I'd like to get back to our hotel..."

Nyland parked the van outside The Shady Lane. "I'll wait," he offered.

"Get as far away from here as possible," Mitsuo insisted. "Leave this country. Start a new life somewhere else."

"To live like Lazarus? What life is there after you've given up your life?"

The Count stepped onto the sidewalk and gazed back at the farmer. "That's the life I've lived for the last half century," he commented enigmatically.

As Nyland drove off, the Count settled on a wooden bench at the door of the pub. Mitsuo went inside to make his call.

"I don't think they'll be long," Mitsuo said, minutes later, coming out. He sat beside the aristocrat and could feel the man's whole body quaking.

"I've been using opium since my son was kidnapped in 1921," the Count told Mitsuo. "They never found the child, and his mother never recovered from the shock. You've seen what a dim light the Countess sheds. As a young mother, she gave off quite a brilliant glow. All that ended when our boy was taken." He stared ahead at nothing at all. "It hasn't been the same since then, you see."

"Life's heavy blows," acknowledged Mitsuo with sympathy.

The Count slipped his arm over the other man's shoulder. "But now I have a son again," he said. "And a fine one at that. I'm really quite a lucky man."

Sick on a Journey

Sick on a journey:
Over parched fields
Dreams wander on.
—Basho

With the Abbot gone to market to sell their excess vegetables, Kanzo, the senior monk, sent a novice rushing to the police station to fetch an officer.

Seeing that an emergency was taking place at the monastery, the newly appointed Chief of Police decided to handle the matter himself. He feared indelicacy on the part of his subordinates. Not to mention that there were only three other officers on duty today. Fukura was a quiet town and seven full-time policemen and three part-time deputies comprised the total force.

The Chief of Police strapped on his revolver and returned to the monastery with the young monk. As they walked—the day, after all was a lovely one and fuel was severely rationed—the policeman attempted to engage the novice in conversation. The officer was splendidly educated and curious about the beliefs of others, to say the least. Perhaps his aim was to examine the fellow's philosophy under his own precision-ground mental lens, and to summarily dispatch an inferior system of ideas. The religious, however, refused to engage in idle chatter. He had already learned this much discipline—a grand knowledge, if compared with that of ordinary men.

By the time they arrived at the simple temple on the edge of a series of fields under cultivation, the Abbot had returned from his business in town. He was, in fact, counting his earnings as the Chief of Police removed his shoes and entered the door. "Ah ha," thought the policeman. "See, I catch him absorbed in his finances, just like any other greedy man. He certainly can't be anything special."

There was a great deal of suspicion recently on the part of the authorities that certain of the religious orders were stirring up anti-government sentiment, as well as committing other crimes. The new appointee had been warned to be on the lookout for activities of that kind. Of course, some people claimed–though never out loud–that the charges against the clergy were really meant to divert attention from a series of misfortunes in the far-flung territories.

The Abbot turned and greeted the two, then sent the young monk on about his chores. He offered the policeman a seat on the tatami and announced his intention of preparing a cup of tea for him.

Although hot and dusty, the law enforcement representative brushed aside that courteous offer. He wasn't here for socializing. "I'll place the thief in custody now," he informed the Abbot. "Tomorrow, I'll send an officer to take a deposition. No need for any of the monks to come to the trial." The man would receive a three-year sentence, the police official calculated.

"There's been an inconvenient error, I'm sorry to say," countered the Abbot. "It's been caused by our stupidity entirely." He smiled cordially and studied the policeman. "I'm quite ashamed. We've brought you all the way out here from town. And walking, too! Please take my bicycle for the ride back. I'll pick it up one day next week, when we go begging."

No thief! Had they gotten him out here just on a whim? How utterly irksome. And as for begging! Here the man was with a stack of bills and coins in front of him. Such an attitude was typical of these sects, the policeman mused. They didn't engage in productive work, but lived idly off the labor of the lower classes, who had been taught an ironclad respect.

"There isn't a thief?" he asked with a sharp look at the Abbot. "I was told a man had broken into the temple."

"How can someone break into a temple–which is never closed?" responded the Abbot mildly. "The doors here merely

132

serve to keep the weather from disturbing our prayers–never to block a fellow creature from gaining shelter."

Oh, how pious! Could anyone really believe such a thing? Grimacing tightly in an expression he hoped might pass for a smile, the policeman bowed. "Please call on me whenever you require, reverend sir. I shall come myself whatever your need. I am Chief of Police Shimazo Satoshi."

"Ahh, a high official," acknowledged the Abbot after digesting the news. "What an honor to our humble temple."

If a title such as Police Chief could move the unworldly monastic to such praise, then Shimazo's full glory would bowl over the man utterly. "Baron Shimazo," the policeman added, trying to suppress a smirk.

"Imagine that, a Baron," admired the Abbot with a heavy sigh, a sufficient display to Satoshi that as a spiritual disciple, the Abbot was simply an old fraud (although possibly not an anti-authority propagandist).

"I will prevail upon you to visit us more often now that you have introduced yourself," added the priest. "Since you are obviously a man of learning, there are many matters I would like to take up with you."

"Certainly," concurred Satoshi, having no plan to attend the Abbot anytime soon.

"I will expect you the day after tomorrow then–for our evening meal at four p.m. Take the bicycle now, if you will be so kind. You can return it to me when you come back."

The head of the monastery dismissed the Baron/Chief of Police as he would any novice–or worse, a servant. He had known many servants in his youth, of course, insomuch as the Abbot–named Hiroaka at his birth–had himself been called Baron Shimazo, once upon a time.

"I thought it best to summon the police when I caught the man combing through our treasures," Kanzo, the senior monk, explained despairingly. He wasn't remorseful in the slightest and considered pitting his will against the Abbot's to be the proper tack to take. The Abbot himself emphasized that material things, too, had their place in the world, and that man must preserve and respect even inanimate objects.

"Our treasures? Combing through our treasures? I don't think he had gotten that far, had he?" asked the Abbot, among who's habits was counted acid sarcasm toward his little flock.

"The precious statues and ritual objects," insisted Kanzo.

"Oh, *those* treasures," replied the Abbot in mock relief. "I thought the man had wormed his way already into our hearts. But certainly not, if you sent for the police to take the fellow away. Hungry was he? Or perhaps ill? Had a family to feed? Calling the police was, by all means, the very best thing for him." With so many national resources tied up in the military infrastructure and in maintenance of a tight control on the territories, there were thousands of destitute peasants wandering the countryside seeking a sustenance living. Their presence everywhere as shadowy, apologetic figures was a hallmark of the time,

"I wasn't concerned with the man's position," admitted the monk, a little less confident now that a shabbier aspect of his own character had been brought into relief. "He's probably lazy, refuses to work," he continued in a more restrained fashion, but still not giving in.

"I'm glad to say that's not *my* problem," put in the Abbot. "I have enough trouble urging a couple of dozen slothful monks to make their best efforts." He softened and smiled kindly at Kanzo. "No harm done. The man is being fed and sent on his way. Unless he'd like to spend the night."

"You tell us to be practical, but when someone tries to steal from us, you refuse to punish him." The monk now genuinely wanted a resolution to that conundrum.

The Abbot snorted. "You desire an easy answer, like a pill for a stomachache? Of course we must defend ourselves, but there isn't a rule about when and where, is there? Once in a while, compassion might seize the upper hand. I'd hardly like to lock compassion out. Would you?"

At last, the monastery head placed the vegetable money with great satisfaction into a tin. "Now we have something for our charitable offerings!"

When Hiroaka had left his estate outside Tokyo, it was with trembling and trepidation. He had been sick with fear to be venturing into the unknown.

That was almost thirty years ago. Today, he was a man of inner certainty and decisiveness. His eyes sparkled and he was on the throes of reviving a once-proud monastery that had–like religion itself–fallen into disfavor during a more outward-seeking period of the country's history.

What had effected such a transformation in the man?

Kyoto had been a city of thriving temples three decades before when Hiroaka had been welcomed by the monks at the Temple of Mercy–an aspect of the Buddha's nature of which Hiroaka very much yearned to be a recipient. His visit there had been arranged by the old merchant who had befriended him, Mr. Nakajima–the only man alive who had heard the then-Baron Shimazo's entire story.

Hiroaka had assuredly not been brought up as a Buddhist, but when the birdseller explained the particular virtues of that religion and the solace that it could grant, the naval officer, badly crippled in his soul, decided to try it. For a sophisticate such as Hiroaka, a graduate of a top British university, such a step was the result of intense despair.

"Namo Ahmida Batsu," chanted the monks, "Namo Ahmida Batsu." They looked toward Buddha as the compassionate one, as well as to his son, the Kwannon deity, who forgave and consoled in the Pure Land of the West.

Hiroaka remained with the monks as a guest, and absorbed the peace that permeated the temple, a serenity born of the constant chanting, the careful movements, and the incense-impregnated walls.

The monks brought Hiroaka his meals for the first few days, then gradually drew him into the life of the community.

135

Initially, he participated just in the work, with the physical labor a balm to his body. Eventually, he joined the prayers, which offered a nourishment for his inner being. He fell into a period of effortless and graceful living.

But there is little easeful about the life of a monk. Comfort, security, and relief from internal struggle are, in fact, irreconcilable with the true spiritual life. These illusory elements feed the existence only of the ordinary man and are sought by him alone. The development of the soul comes through extreme exertion and agitation, a waking up to the primacy of the needs of the spirit, a willingness to sacrifice everything to this pursuit.

One day, a certain Itami Shiki arrived on foot from Osaka. He was on pilgrimage and had vowed to visit one thousand temples in order to hear the teaching at each and to determine at which place he must eventually settle down. Shiki was consumed by his thirst for the Buddha's awakening.

Hiroaka had sought merely inner harmony, a goal that Shiki scorned completely. "Why eat a bowl of mealy worms, when you can have fine white rice?" the young contemplative asked the nobleman. "Why stay here, where there is nothing that will release you from the wheel of birth and rebirth to this life of suffering? By that I mean there is no master at this temple who can show the way."

Hiroaka was amazed that a seeker required a master to teach Truth, or that there was possible a change in state so revolutionary that it would free a sentient being forever from the law of karma–or what the Western philosophers called cause and effect.

When Shiki prepared to leave for the remote villages, Hiroaka packed up what was now a single sackful of belongings, and followed along. The Merciful One had granted him this boon–that he could hear the tinkling of a distant bell.

"The thief requests an audience with you," the senior monk informed his Roshi.

"Hasn't the man a name?" retorted the Abbot with a

penetrating glance at his student.

"I'm sure he must, but I didn't ask it, not wanting to encourage too close an association with someone like him."

"Do you fear the company of your fellow men?" inquired the Abbot more quietly.

"You have taught us to avoid those who are low in nature." This was half a question from the senior monk.

"It is best that we avoid low places, for, indeed, their influence might do us harm, but even that precept can hardly be an absolute for men who pursue the gate to freedom. As for shunning the company of those whose natures might be corrupting to us, this is a praiseworthy guidance–but only applicable to the disciple who can discern a man of lower worth from one of value and esteem. If your only counsel in selecting the radiant from the infernal is a man's clothes or even his actions, I think you'd better accept all men as equals, and treat each one as circumspectly as the other." The speech was a long one for the Abbot, who spoke economically outside a weekly instruction to his monks. "Bring the man in, I'll have a word with him."

The thief, whatever his name was (Hajime, perhaps) entered the Abbot's private room and bowed before him in great humility. The Abbot, having spent the last 30 years or so observing human nature (his own for a start), was nowise fooled by this display. He bowed to Hajime equally deeply, echoing the thief's intention to deceive.

Hajime jumped back, startled. "Eh? What's that?" he asked.

"You requested a conference with me?" prodded the Abbot.

"Yes, yes, your holiness. I can't tell you how grateful I am for all that you've done."

"Good," agreed the Abbot. "Then you mustn't. But tell me this. What will you do with yourself after today?"

"I'm a completely reformed man," declared the thief with a saccharine sincerity.

"Oh, what good a meal and a little kindness can do," responded the Abbot dryly.

"Yes, reverend one." Here, Hajime believed he was on firmer ground.

"Go then and sin no more," advised the Abbot, who often read the Christian Bible.

"That I will, sir. First off, I'll find a job."

"That would be suitable," concurred the Abbot, in all seriousness. "And I must give you a single admonition before you go. If you adhere to my advice, your place in Heaven is assured."

Even a man like Hajime must be curious as to what such guidance might be. "Yes? What then?"

"Never allow a habit to seize hold of you. Before you undertake any task, ask yourself first: `Have I done this before? Do I need to do this thing now? Do I do this out of habit?' If you will follow this simple prescription, you will be saved."

The man bowed, stood, and backed away from the Abbot.

Kanzo, the senior student, appeared from nowhere and led the man away. An afternoon period of chanting and meditation was not far off.

Returned a minute later to confront his Abbot, Kanzo asked. "Sir, why give the thief advice of that nature, that whatever he does, it should simply not be from habit? How will that assure this man's redemption?"

"Ahh," considered the Abbot. "As foolish a man as he seemed–as utterly without hope of going anywhere in his life but to jail, I can assure you that Hajime's essential self is shaped very much similarly to your own. Don't mistake me in what I say to you, Kanzo. All men are not alike inside themselves, but this man has an essence of some purity. He chose to be reborn as he was for many reasons. The predominant purpose, it could be, was to find his way here, to this temple."

The senior monk chewed over these concepts. Assuredly, he could never quite grasp what his Abbot was implying. Kanzo paused, knowing that the Abbot would go on if the student were silent.

"But the man's whole difficulty, and this is merely a matter of character"–the Abbot appeared to feel a man's character was of little moment–"is that he is habituated to theft. He sees himself as a thief and acts on that assumption always and only. The man is no more a thief than you are."

Kanzo reddened.

"But he has the habit of those actions. So I spoke truly when I said to him that if he could break all habits of his, he would be saved–that is, on the road to transformation." The Abbot shook his head in some weariness. "Such a thing is easier suggested than achieved. I don't expect a change in him. Although odder things happen among us humankind."

"How is it that you know such mysteries, Master?"

"How is it that you do not?"

With Shiki, Hiroaka went from temple to temple, staying only so long in each as to be considered simply passing through. Shiki was so concentrated on pursing his enlightenment that he had no time for the rigors of communal life. In fact, even Hiroaka, who had been supported by his family from birth without having had to lift a finger, was discomforted by living completely off the generosity of the various religious compounds. He resolved to cut himself loose from Shiki at the next opportunity, and to wander on alone.

At least one thing was true for Hiroaka finally–he was no longer afraid of every sound, of every movement in the brush. Being out in the world, of itself, had soothed many of his terrors, had broken the back of his multiple obsessions by complex distractions as much as anything else.

Their next stop was an unpretentious roadside shrine housing a poor, middle-aged monk, who reluctantly shared a few grains of rice with his visitors. Hiroaka refused, however, to partake of the man's meager meal.

"My friend here is a Baron. He's accustomed to much

daintier fare than this," teased Shiki, who dug in, ate, then watched carefully to see if their host was going to finish every scrap of his own half-bowlful.

The monk stopped eating. "A Baron? Sincerely?"

Hiroaka blushed. He had met so many fine men in the last few months, most of them poor from birth and very likely to remain that way. "I am, but I have made up my mind to renounce my title so that it and the estates can pass to my son."

The monk scrutinized the young Baron judiciously. "Bravely done and with what fatherly sentiment. Is there much property involved?"

"Oh, quite a bit. I'm not sure of the specifics..."

"I salute you," replied the monk.

Shiki continued his journey in the morning, leaving Hiroaka behind to decide his next step. Their host urged Hiroaka to stay one more day and promised that he would later give him directions to a temple where he might remain for a while. In the meantime, the monk went about his daily business.

Hiroaka, having grown somewhat used to a routine of chanting and prayer, sat before the shrine to the Lord Buddha and burned a stick of fragrant incense. Shiki had told Hiroaka that he would gain neither enlightenment nor merit from such actions as these–since only a radical insight into Reality would tear off the blinders. But, added Shiki, prayer and meditation would probably do Hiroaka no harm. At any rate, as the aristocrat was unlikely to ever go further than he had already come, there was no danger to him at all from these practices.

Hiroaka, therefore, still fasting from the day before, prayed from hunger-spurred passion. With starvation a goad to his emotional reaching toward the Buddha and Kwannon, Hiroaka decided to go without food for another day or two and to concentrate on his meditations.

The monk-attendant of the sanctuary returned. He had brought a fish for both of them to eat. "As your traveling companion mentioned that you are used to better provisions, I will prepare a fit meal for you."

Hiroaka protested, but it was true he was hungry. How rude he would be to deny the monk the opportunity of offering hospitality. With some sense of relief, Hiroaka accepted the unsought kindness.

After a while, the fine feast was served. The fish was delicious and plentiful, and good quality white rice accompanied it. The monk nodded and smiled and served Hiroaka some more. The monk partook of only the rice, saving the fish for his company. Hiroaka ate his fill.

As the food began to break down in his body, a nightmarish sensation took control of the young Baron from head to toe. He reclined on the tatami mat, complaining of his tingling limbs. Hiroaka fell into a swirling maelstrom, a dark hollow inside himself that contained every horror he had undergone at sea and on that desert isle in the Philippines.

"Namo Ahmida Batsu," he whispered until his voice gave way entirely, and then he recited the words inside his head. "Salutations to the Buddha. Namo Ahmida Batsu."

Hiroaka's host rested nonchalantly on his mat, writing on a plain white paper and ignoring the sick man a few feet away.

Finally, he came to the stricken man's side, bearing the document he had drawn up. "Sign this while you still can, Baron Shimazo. This will cede your properties to your son."

Through blurring vision, Hiroaka tried to read the words. Nowhere on the paper could he see his son's name written. Instead, he comprehended that his baronial estates would be granted to the Temple of Earthly Compassion, on the grounds of which he now lay ailing. Hiroaka made no attempt to grasp for the pen. Namo Ahmida Batsu, he prayed. Protect Satoshi and his inheritance!

"Here then, Baron. Can you not move? In a few minutes, you will suffocate. It's sadly true. I've fed you a dish of fugu, leaving in the liver with all its poison. What a mistake! I have tried to serve you a treat and have wound up paralyzing your nervous system. Lord Buddha, if he exists in this realm, will forgive me, I'm sure, since I will carry on this work in his name.

What have you offered to the world so far, Baron Shimazo? Have you been more than a parasite?" The monk continued to hold out the paper and the pen.

So this was the end! Hiroaka was indeed doomed to die. The last period of his life had been full of tribulation, but the lives of most men, he had perceived in his travels, were difficult from birth to death. He had no regrets–well, perhaps that he could not have seen his son again!

Chief of Police Shimazo Satoshi entered the monastery on the day and at the hour he had been bidden to appear. His arrival here was almost a complete surprise to himself. He had planned on sending an officer in his place with the bicycle, but hadn't gotten around to making the arrangement. All right, the Abbot might be annoying, but what was the harm? And what if the man *were* an arch propagandist? Or, worse still, a terrorist, such as had been threatening the public peace in Tokyo? Must Satoshi not then gain an acquaintance with him?

For some reason or other, at the last minute, Satoshi had picked up a scroll to present to the Abbot–a bit of calligraphy in his grandfather's hand, the writing signifying the inexplicable and miraculous nature of life. Satoshi imagined that the monks would appreciate it. He had only brought it to his post at Fukura out of a sentimental attachment to items from home.

The Abbot was remarkably touched by the gift and hung it in a niche at once. "How true, how true, and from your grandfather's own brush. A lively style, wouldn't you say?"

Satoshi had thought there was something boringly traditional about the work and he barely ever glanced at it. "My grandfather was Prime Minister for a time," he replied idly, for something to say.

"Ah then, there must be some value to it."

Satoshi immediately regretted bringing the thing. Now the Abbot translated the art into dollars and cents! Unbelievable!

The Chief of Police sat with the monks for their evening meal. Rice and pickles–truly nothing worthy of a guest. How amazing. And not a word spoken by any of them! Why then invite an outsider to this?

"A satisfying repast," declared the Abbot when the monks had withdrawn. "How glad we are to have had you with us tonight."

Satoshi glanced nervously out toward the portico. A storm was near. If he departed right away, perhaps he might avoid the worst of it.

"Come then and sit in my room with me. I wanted to consult you on various matters."

"Perhaps another time...the weather..."

"Yes," agreed the Abbot. "We're going to have quite a rain in a minute. That's good for the farmers. They've needed it. No use in your rushing off immediately. You're bound to get soaked. We've an extra room for travellers, of course, and welcome you to spend the night."

Why did Satoshi feel so trapped? These monks were harmless, essentially. He followed the Abbot into his living quarters and sat as instructed.

"Tell me first, how it is that you have come to Fukura–a man as important as you, in such an unimportant place."

This irked Satoshi. "I have a mentor in the police–a general. He's sent me here in order that I might gain the rank of chief. After a short while, I'll move on to a more visible post." He wasn't a man beset by ego, but being thought of as having been shunted aside didn't suit him, either.

"Oh, so you'll be on to bigger and better. I am glad for you. Fukura is such a backwater. But tell me why a Baron joins the police ranks, anyway."

"My family has always served the Emperor. My grandfather, as I told you before, was Prime Minister. My father was a naval officer and was lost at sea."

"Lost at sea, was he?" the Abbot exclaimed. "How sad. A boy without his father. What a deprivation. Your father's dead then?"

"Yes," acknowledged Satoshi. "He gave his life for the

Emperor during the war."

This fact gave the Abbot some pause for thought. Perhaps he was considering the futility of man's aggressions.

"What was it you wanted my advice concerning?" questioned Satoshi. He could hear the rain gushing from the heavens at last. Perhaps it was just as well that he hadn't set off a few minutes before.

"Since the war, all interest in religion on the part of our young people has dropped off steeply. What do you suppose might be done to bring them back to their spiritual roots?"

"You're looking for financial support of the monastery, I suppose," responded Satoshi after a moment. What in the world had the Abbot in mind? What did a policeman know of such things? Or it could be that the man was seeking a personal donation–or even complicity in some swindle!

"There are many temples and monasteries in ruins across this area," commented the Abbot. "We have seen the fine structures in Kyoto turned into government offices and military barracks." The Abbot's eyes glowed with an odd fervor. "Although I believe we have done well for ourselves here. I've as many monks in residence today as we did before the war. I wasn't here then, of course, but I do have the records. We've rebuilt somewhat in the last decade. How might Japan itself reconstruct interest in the pietistic side of life, which has all but withered away in our benighted country?"

"The revival of faith would be something you know best," replied the policeman. "Perhaps you have your own opinion there."

The Abbot smiled. "I have several thoughts on this matter, that is true."

Satoshi was more nonplused than ever, having no idea why the Abbot had engaged him thus.

At just this juncture, the temple's senior monk appeared in the doorway. "There's a visitor for you, Master," he advised his superior woodenly.

The Abbot arose and, instructing the monk to see to their

honored guest's needs, went out.

"Some tea, perhaps?" asked the senior monk doubtfully. He surely thought Satoshi must have had enough food and drink for the evening.

"Your Abbot is an unusual man," observed Satoshi, after refusing the offer.

The senior monk's face lightened considerably. "Remarkable, isn't he? How lucky we've been. Perhaps there's one or two to every age. Our Master Tatsuya is the one for this place and time. So you've noticed! I'm glad."

To be sure, Satoshi had seen nothing extraordinary in the Abbot, unless there was a particular talent to getting on a person's nerves. Satoshi nodded sagely, however, and the monk departed, glowing in an outsider's praise of his Roshi.

The Abbot returned with Hajime the thief, who was soaked to the skin from the foul night's effects. Seeing the policeman, Hajime appeared about to flee, but the Abbot stopped him. "This poor man has been out and about in the driving rain. He wisely decided to seek shelter with us," explained the Abbot to Satoshi.

"I needn't stay," whispered the thief nervously. "I didn't know you had company."

The policeman examined Hajime with a perturbed look. He had seen the man somewhere–not a sketch on a `wanted' poster–or could it be?

"I'm certain you won't mind sharing the guest chamber with this man; it's not a proper night to turn someone out!" The Abbot had not for a moment ceased to exhibit his pleasant manner of solicitousness for Satoshi's well-being.

"No, of course. I have no objection," answered the policeman immediately. Did he mind! Most positively he did! If the rain let up even a drop or two, he would dash for home. The man was... unkempt, to say the least. He didn't like the fellow at all!

The Abbot was gratified at that response. Tea was brought in, and the Abbot and Satoshi pursued their unsatisfactory conversation while Hajime gulped at the hot brew and shifted his uncomprehending gaze from one speaker to the next.

Hiroaka lay unable to move although his mind remained as clear as a bell. What a strange state this was!

"It doesn't matter," the monk who had poisoned him assured Hiroaka maliciously. "I will sign your name to the will and bring forth witnesses that you assigned your property to me. There's no lack of those willing to be of service when I call on them. I'm well-liked around these parts, and can easily explain the situation."

Hiroaka urgently tried to clear his throat. Was his airway becoming obstructed already? It seemed only a few weeks ago that he had been as young as his child Satoshi, playing about his own father's knee. And that splendid house! What a shame if it should go to the man who killed him.

And yet, a person's fate was governed not by himself, but by a universal law that moved as clockwork, inexorably.

Unless that man had found liberation.

Hiroaka dwelled on such thoughts as these and very nearly forgot about his tormentor—and even his near-death condition. He barely noticed the appearance of another man, a second monk, who peered down at Hiroaka in unruffled surprise. "What's wrong with this man, brother? Perhaps I can help."

"We had a modest meal and then he collapsed," said the poisoner, his eyes now filled with conjured tears. "Buddha forgive me if his illness was caused by anything I've done."

The second monk felt Hiroaka's limbs and began to massage them. "He's cold. Let's restore the circulation. How about a cover to warm him further?" Briskly, the stranger took charge, kneading at the sick man with the fingers of a skilled physician, pressing on his chest to keep his breath afloat, and generally coaxing Hiroaka back to life.

The first monk wrung his hands at every turn and pointed out that the task was hopeless. If the second man would run for a physician, Hiroaka might have a greater chance to live.

This comedy went on for perhaps an hour, until the second monk had Hiroaka up and flopping his feet on the ground, trying to regain some muscular control. As soon as Hiroaka could swallow, too, at least a gallon of water was poured into him.

Had the monk had any special training? the would-be killer inquired, eager to pry the man's fingers away from his "charge."

Perhaps some, the helper admitted modestly. As head of a monastery, he was often called upon to try many skills.

The second monk was so very self-assured that Hiroaka gained confidence. He might not die yet, after all. The murderous monk was chagrined, nervous, exasperated, and, finally, left to fetch a physician, and never returned.

The stranger stayed more than a week, feeding Hiroaka broth and stories of enlightenment. That man was Tatsuya I, later Hiroaka's master, and his predecessor at the Temple of the Golden Dawn.

Sometimes the path picks a disciple up by his heels and gives him a shake—a gentle, welcoming love pat to the adherent.

Satoshi was an early riser. The moment he sensed the break of day, he hopped up from the futon, thrusting one leg into his pants. The rain had stopped. The futon opposite, not yet rolled up for the day, was nonetheless empty. This Hajime—what was he wanted for, anyway? or was that only a mistake on Satoshi's part?—had probably gone out in obedience to nature's summons.

The Police Chief pulled on the rest of his clothes, feeling rather too disheveled for his station in life. He reached into his pocket for his watch. Not there. Well then, where had he left it? He searched among the bedclothes, then everywhere else!

The watch was expensive, American-made. A friend of his mother's, Count Asano, had bought it for Satoshi while on a trade mission. Damn! Chief of Police Shimazo's blood began to simmer. His roommate for the night had made off with his watch!

As prompt as Satoshi was in following the sun's example, in terms of the temple's rhythms, he was late. The monks were already at their worship when he burst out of his little room. He tiptoed past the meditation hall. The door was open, giving him a view of several dozen or so backs. Joining the monks in meditation were seekers from the town. The senior student rang a bell and a chant began.

Satoshi tried to allow the atmosphere of the ceremony to reach inside and soothe him. It would shame the nobleman if the switch occurred the other way around–if those in prayer became subject to his agitation. He found his shoes in the rack by the door, then sat on the porch and put them on. The morning was a fine one. Too bad his humor had been ruined by the missing timepiece, but there it was. He was disturbed by its loss and swore never to visit the temple again.

Just as Satoshi was ready to begin a fast-paced walk back to the station, the Abbot appeared on the path beside him.

"I didn't want you to get away without my biding you farewell, Satoshi," said the priest familiarly.

A presumptuous salutation, Satoshi thought. "My watch is gone," he blurted out. "A good one, too, brought to me from America!"

The two men stood for a while, observing one another. Satoshi had hoped to elicit some reaction of responsibility–at least commiseration–from the Abbot, but the Abbot merely continued to regard the policeman.

"Come back into the temple. I have something for you," he finally told Satoshi in a noncommittal tone.

Desiring to witness some more volatile emotion on his own behalf, Satoshi meekly followed the priest inside.

In his quarters, the Abbot unwrapped something from a scrap of silk brocade. There on the richly patterned, rose material sat a man's wristwatch. "It's for you," the Abbot assured Satoshi. "I'm glad you've come for it. I've wound it every day for the last 42 years. I never wear the watch, of course. There is no place for watches here. How lucky I am that you've reminded me."

Satoshi took the piece of jewelry into his hand. The watch was an antique–gold, made in England, 17 jeweled, with the initials SH on the back alongside the date, 1934.

"But whose watch is this?" Satoshi asked, his anger turned to curiosity.

"A man who died here a long time ago," the Abbot said. "A young man, a bit foolish, proud of his birth, filled with conceit and theories of every kind–a belief in honor and justice and so on, and so on. A tiresome man, really, a very limited, commonplace type."

Satoshi frowned. "Honor and justice? Do you disapprove of those?"

"Very much so. Certainly," concurred the Abbot. "A man for whom honor and justice are necessary will, on the turn of a wheel, become dishonorable and unjust in the name of their opposites. He'll go so far as to wage war on those who oppose him. Thousands will die in honor's name."

"Perhaps you're right," Satoshi relented. "But I can't accept the watch, of course."

"You must," insisted the Abbot. "This isn't a social gesture on my part, believe me. And it's quite possible that I won't see you again."

"Oh, surely I'll come back," objected Satoshi. "Perhaps you'll have another thief." He smiled.

"The earth revolves and we will all be in a different place by tomorrow," replied the older man.

Satoshi placed the watch on his wrist, bowed, and departed for a second time that morning.

Kanzo entered and turned on the desk lamp for the Abbot, who stopped writing to remark, "I don't really need that. The light from the hall is good enough." At 11 at night, he was still figuring the monastery's accounts. In another five hours he would be the first one in the meditation hall.

"I was about to go to sleep and turn the hall light out."

"That's all right then," agreed Hiroaka. Last month's

electricity bill had been particularly grievous. Gone were the days when monks could live on rice and tea.

Kanzo remained standing by the Abbot's side.

"Something you want to tell me?" asked the Master.

"Where is the lesson in the theft of the watch? Will Hajime be stricken with remorse and return here as a monk? Will the policeman find a revelation in this?"

The Abbot laughed quietly. There were men sleeping on the other side of the thin partition. "Hajime the thief is lost to us," said Hiroaka. "We placed the bait on our hook, but he failed to bite. In taking the watch, he passed up everything he might have gained. Do you know Shakespeare? `He who steals my purse steals trash.'"

The story of Othello was the perfect example of men so caught up in their identification with the "I" that they would destroy anything to fulfill their driving passions–mere temporal impulses, rooted only in the outer structure of personality.

"Why wouldn't you have known from the beginning, Master, that this would be the outcome?"

"Sometimes I know things; sometimes I don't. I'm not a magician, Kanzo, only a man. I know what I need to know, that's all. Our aim here isn't to realize everything that goes on in the human domain."

"And the policeman? Will he be your student now?"

"He hasn't a particle of possibility. Didn't you see that? A nice young man though. On the whole that is," he amended. "By a certain ordinary standard."

Kanzo made to go, but the Abbot's voice arrested him. "I wish I could see much better from the rest of you, however. Those of you who have the potential and who fritter it away. If none of you is going to work, I shall be forced to close the monastery. This isn't a rest home. Think of the farmers whose money we take. We're supposed to be working for their salvation."

Kanzo was struck to the core with a pang of guilt. Had he, or had he not, made his sincerest effort of late?

"My old friend Shiki comes to us on Friday for a week or two. Let him work where he can do so most easily. He has arthritis in both knees, poor man. You remember him, of course, from his visit last summer. There's my idea of wasted opportunity. For years, he ran from temple to temple, hearing every vaunted teaching, but latching on to none. Without a master, he's snuck through life, escaping having the dharma applied to him. But the Buddha's philosophy serves as well for manure, if it's not practiced. Don't you think so, Kanzo?"

The senior monk was sure of nothing tonight. "I'll bring you a glass of water, Master, and turn off the other light."

In Blood-Red Cataracts

Ua Mau Ke Ea O Ka Aina I Ka Pono (The life of the land is perpetuated in rightness.)
–King Kamehameha III

Commander Hideo Fuchida strolled down the wharf toward the sentry point. The air was warm and humid, but a strong breeze blew into Hilo from Onomea to the west, carrying with it the perfume of plumeria blossoms.

No, perhaps Fuchida was wrong. Maybe he was just smelling the Pacific beyond.

Lulled by the rhythm of each successive wave that tried to overwhelm the Imperial Japanese battery on the Big Island, Hawaii, Fuchida failed to hear the step behind him on the planking. If he had heard it, however, he would only have been expecting one of his own. The Japanese were well ensconced in the Islands by now, ever since, in fact, the scuttling of a dozen vessels along Battleship Row, Pearl Harbor, more than five decades before. The 1949 treaty with the so-called Allied forces had only sealed a *fait accompli*.

Fuchida paused to light a cigarette before moving on. The Islands were beautiful, but he yearned for Hiroshima, his home. With his mind occupied in calculating retirement benefits for all the years of service to his Emperor, Fuchida was bewildered by a strong hand clasping his mouth, pulling back his head.

This could not be happening to him!

So confused were his thoughts, that Commander Fuchida barely felt the sting of the razor's edge severing the delicate and vital tissues of his throat.

Anne Glasgow was just rising from the bed of Deputy Inspector Takeo Tanizaki. "Wait ten minutes and I'll drive you home in the jeep," Tanizaki proposed.

"No. It only invites family arguments." She reached for her dress.

Tanizaki shook his head. "That brother of yours..." he began. Then he got out of bed as well and put on his pants.

"Oh, it isn't simply Perry, you know. It's all of them."

Tanizaki snorted in derision. "But why? It's been such a long time. So many of the people here were already of Japanese ancestry. The Hawaiians always have been racially mixed. Look at you." He obeyed his own suggestion and regarded her evaluatively. There was only a hint of Polynesian antecedents in her face. Her brother Perry, the rebel, by contrast, looked almost sheer Hawaiian. Anne had held onto the Glasgow's Scottish/Irish genes.

"I don't disagree with you," Anne answered him. "But not everyone here feels the same way." She gave Tanizaki a caustic smile, having stated the obvious.

Tanizaki hesitated. "Commander Fuchida was killed last night," he informed her.

"Yes. They were talking about it at the bank today. Nothing ever happens here, so we just must have our gossip. I suppose you're part of the investigation?" Anne was almost ready to go, running her fingers through her hair, glancing into the mirror high over the chest of drawers that held nearly all of the policeman's wardrobe.

Tanizaki considered lying, but what was the point? Everyone knew everything in Hilo—not so large a town as it had been before the occupation. *Reannexation*, Tanizaki corrected in his own mind. The Americans had never belonged in Asia anyway. The Japanese had liberated the Hawaiian Islands.

"Baron Shimazo, *Colonel* Shimazo that is, is in charge. I'm only the Emperor's footsoldier, you realize. I've been questioning some of the known provocateurs." Tanizaki's eyes wouldn't quite meet Anne's.

She picked up her purse. "Do you enjoy that, Takeo?" she asked astringently, moving past him on her way to the door.

154

He stopped her, put his hands around her waist and pulled her closer. "Things aren't the way they were forty years ago—with interrogation. We're trying to cultivate the masses now, not decimate them."

Sooner or later he would have to get around to Perry Glasgow, that was obvious. Although Perry worked for the Japanese government managing a sleepy branch of the post office in Kona, Anne's brother was a known dissident. Tanizaki couldn't understand why. Glasgow was Polynesian—that is, an original Hawaiian. Why would a man like that feel loyalty to an America that had dominated the Islands, obliterated the culture, and had been vanquished from the Pacific since long before either of them was born?

Tanizaki was about to hand Perry's name over to his assistant, Junichiro, and have Perry brought to the stationhouse. Then he thought the better of it.

The order from the Pacific Command, and the reason why Baron Shimazo had been sent here so recently, was to use greater restraint with the native groups. The reform government in New Edo was trying to turn the situation around in the protectorates—win the population over and finally end the guerilla skirmishes that too often cost Japanese lives in Hawaii, Guam, Micronesia, the Marianas, and the Philippines.

Tanizaki steered his jeep toward the Kona District where he easily found a parking place. So few of the Islanders had cars, these days. The economy was a poor one, despite the millions of yen in military dollars the parent country pumped into the region annually.

The Imperial soldier guarding the post office exterior saluted Tanizaki, who merely grunted. Despite Tanizaki's uniform, and even though his salary was paid by the Ministry of Defense, the detective hardly regarded himself as belonging to the Army.

Perry was working at one of the windows. He was busy selling a money order to a Polynesian woman. As the woman pulled her money from inside her bra, she exposed half her breast, then laughed at her "accident." Tanizaki was disgusted. Sometimes he wondered at the level of these people.

Perry blushed and looked away, his eyes meeting Tanizaki's with a jolt of recognition. Of course he knew who Tanizaki was. "They" all knew who the Japanese officers were on the Big Island–the Island of Hawaii–no matter how unimportant.

Tanizaki signaled to Glasgow to come away for a talk, and a heavyset Hawaiian woman took over at the window. Perry led the detective into a back storeroom where piles of letters awaited processing by the Japanese Board of Censors.

"How's my sister?" asked Perry before Tanizaki had a chance to set the tone for the interview.

Tanizaki ignored him. "Commander Fuchida was murdered on the docks the other night."

"So I heard. Right under the eyes of the sentry on duty. Very regrettable, of course." Perry grinned and leaned against a stack of mail.

"You are a member of the Hawaiian-Americans Alliance," Tanizaki observed sharply. Perry Glasgow's color changed. "I'm not here as a Political Officer, Glasgow," Tanizaki continued smugly. "My only interest is in bringing Fuchida's killer to justice."

"I didn't have anything to do with that," Perry mumbled, disconcerted.

Tanizaki reached over and grabbed the man's shoulder, then shook him roughly. "But you know who did!" the Japanese officer shouted in the postal employee's face.

"No. No, I don't," Perry yelled back. He yanked away from Tanizaki and shoved him, but when Perry realized what he had done, and to whom, he blenched. Only a few years before, Tanizaki might have taken Perry out and had him shot immediately for such an offense.

The two men stared at one another. "Well?" demanded Tanizaki. He was pleased that Perry had lost control; it gave him a strong opening.

"Ask the kahuna 'ana'ana," Perry whispered.

A feeling of exultation rose up in the deputy inspector. He had hit pay dirt, as the Americanism went. Tanizaki nodded sagely, knowingly. He had no idea what Perry meant, but Anne would tell him. "The kahuna 'ana'ana," he repeated to himself, lest he forget.

Who the hell was the kahuna 'ana'ana? he wondered. "The kahuna 'ana'ana, isn't one exact person," Anne laughed. "A kahuna is a priest with a lot of mana, you know. A kahuna 'ana'ana is someone who prays his victim to death, usually at the chief's request." She lay next to Tanizaki, running her hand down his long, muscular thigh.

"Some sort of sorcerer," he exclaimed in annoyance. "How stupid. Fuchida wasn't cursed to death. The man had his throat slit. This was no supernatural incident."

"Maybe not," conceded Anne. "But nowadays a kahuna needs all the help he can get. Fuchida was disliked intensely here. He was responsible for a lot of misery. No one on the Big Island is mourning his death."

Tanizaki had not exactly been a fan of Fuchida's himself. Fuchida had chastised him personally on more than one occasion for "leniency" toward the populace. The Commander had represented the old guard in his relationships with the Hawaiian people. He had been behind the "disappearance" of many young men, and even some women.

An act of this nature, however, could not be overlooked. The Commander's murder was rebellion and a threat to the Japanese rule of the Islands.

Tanizaki lay there quietly for a while. "Where do I find the kahuna 'ana'ana?" he asked finally.

"All right. I'll take you," Anne replied. "Tomorrow. We'll drive to Kilauea."

"The volcano?" He was startled, didn't understand.

"Yes, the fire pit. The goddess Pele's home. It has always

been an important place of worship."

Tanizaki sat up. "What do you mean, 'worship?' The Hawaiian Islanders are Christians, aren't they?"

"On the surface, we are," Anne acknowledged with a half-smile. "But our traditional religion lies right under that."

Even the jeep could only go so far before they had to get out and walk. "Is this all lava formation?" asked Tanizaki, poking at the ground with a hardwood walking stick.

"Yes," Anne agreed. "Hawaii is only incidentally a chain of islands. We're actually living on mountains that have thrust up from the ocean floor."

"It's beautiful here," he reflected. "Quite a paradise, to be trite." Exotic orchids dotted the profuse vegetation carpeting the forest.

"A lava flow," Anne exclaimed, pointing at a molten brew creeping across a ridge not far from where they climbed.

"Is it dangerous out here?" Tanizaki questioned nervously. Anne didn't answer. A sudden flume of steam and the stench of sulfur told him that the earth under them was as restless as a wild beast.

A rattling in the brush brought Tanizaki to a standstill and he motioned at Anne to follow his example. On her instruction, he had stored his pistol at home, and he was left clutching his wooden stick as a weapon.

Anne's brother Perry popped out of the undergrowth. *Perry? What was he doing here?*

"Didn't get too early a start, did you?" Perry grumbled, seemingly heedless of Tanizaki's flicker of discomfort and fear.

She had set him up. She saw him as the enemy.

Anne took Tanizaki's arm and he flinched involuntarily. "What's wrong?" she asked. "It's only Perry. We'll go on a little farther now."

Turning back made no sense, of course. Whatever Anne and Perry were intent on doing, they were going to carry out regardless of any protest on his part, or any attempt to return to

Hilo.

"The old Hawaiians practiced human sacrifice, didn't they?" asked Tanizaki directly and defiantly. "They threw their victims into the volcanos."

"Don't be silly," Anne refuted, leading him on. "They buried the dead that way, that's all. I mean, cremated them. But no living sacrifice, that I've ever heard of."

They continued to ascend.

"We're almost at the crater," Perry announced. "Pele's home. The place of big mana. Can you feel the power of the goddess, Tanizaki?"

The Japanese shook his head, disregarding the question. Out of the corner of his eye he spotted a girl dressed all in white. He turned, but the sylph had vanished.

"What did you see?" demanded Anne, who had been watching him.

"A woman. Are there people up here?"

Perry and Anne turned to look at one another. "There are kahunas nearby–priests–but no wahines. No women, except Pele. That's who you saw."

Tanizaki smiled at them grimly. "If you say so," he retorted in irritation.

"It's a good omen," Anne announced, satisfied with her own explanation. "Pele likes you."

Tanizaki poked at the burnt, ashy earth with his stick.

"A little further," Perry encouraged, moving on.

When the three at last planted themselves at the rim of the caldron, they peered over onto a bed of fire. Scorching, sulfurous vapors bit at Tanizaki's throat, forcing him to cough. He waited for Perry and Anne to thrust at him, push him over the edge into the deity Pele's hungering mouth. He rooted himself as best he could, as he had been taught by his sensei, his martial arts teacher, at home.

Anne pulled a package from her purse and handed it to Perry, who dropped it into the volcano's maw. Tanizaki tensed as she seized hold of his arm. "A present for Pele," she said.

"Let's go back down the slope."

They stumbled into what he believed was a settlement, but what Anne informed him was a region of monuments dedicated to the gods. Low, rock walls surrounded ground paved with sea-smoothed stones, forming a series of individual shrines. In the center of each stood one-, two-, and even three-storied timber altars. On the first story of each "tower" was a platform. "For offerings," Anne explained in a low voice. Carved wooden images of the divine persons (the akua) were scattered all around.

The visitors sat on a great outcropping of lava and as Tanizaki's eyes gradually adjusted to the dimming sun, he perceived that the three of them were not alone. Kahunas were busily engaged in a variety of tasks—building a fire, preparing for a ritual. A chill ran up and down Tanizaki's spine. These figures had appeared wraithlike out of the mist. Had they been there all along? Were they men? The Japanese, much like the Hawaiians, were susceptible to thoughts of ghosts.

The fire was lit. One of the kahunas knelt by Perry and spoke to him in soft tones and unfamiliar words. "Have you seen hula?" Perry asked the Japanese policeman.

"Yes, of course," Tanizaki declared. "We have hula at the officers' luaus."

Anne smiled as if her lover had said something foolish, then she gazed into the distance.

"No," disagreed Perry sardonically. "Real hula. Ritual hula. Performed by the dancer in a dream state."

Tanizaki regarded Perry. "Why would you and Anne bring me up here—conspire to bring me up here, I should say—to show me what you call `real hula'?"

"Because my sister likes you," Perry answered with a wicked, cutting smile.

"Because we are going to hand Fuchida's killer over to you," Anne corrected. "And then you will see luakini, human sacrifice."

The package they had thrown into Kilauea had been a lock of Commander Fuchida's hair, they told Tanizaki. They had prayed to Pele to remove the Japanese occupiers from her sacred islands and she had asked for such a token. But the one who had performed the act in Pele's name knew, as they all had known, that the Japanese would not allow the murder of the Commander to go unpunished.

The killer was to be another gift to Pele. He would be "executed" for his crime, and Tanizaki would be a witness to that act. The Japanese authorities would thus be satisfied with their solution of the homicide, as would Pele with the blood sacrifice. She would grant the peoples' prayers.

No, they didn't say these words directly to his face, telling him that he and his masters were unwelcome here, but he was not a stupid man, and he understood what their explanation meant.

One of the kahunas brought out a Polynesian boy named David Kalakaua. "Are you guilty of the murder of the Japanese Commander?" Perry asked the young man, tonelessly.

"Yes," agreed the teenager.

Perry displayed a statement written in both Japanese and English describing exactly how David had killed the Commander. David, the statement noted, had held a deep anger at Fuchida; he blamed the Commander for the disappearance of his father two years before.

The boy signed.

Had David Kalakaua actually murdered Fuchida? Tanizaki debated, or had the guilt been "assigned" to him by the Hawaiian-Americans Alliance? The detective watched the boy's every move with utmost care, but could not decide. Both David and Perry were devoid of emotion as they clarified for Tanizaki what the boy had done and how he must be punished under their own law, in their own way.

Sulfur fumes drifted down the mountainside and Tanizaki choked again and again.

"I cannot allow it," he finally gasped. "I must take David back to Hilo for a proper police examination. I insist that this be done in accordance with Japanese law, the law of this land."

The four of them sat silently for a moment, engaging in a contest of wills. Tanizaki concentrated on relaxing his throat soas not to betray weakness with another cough.

"Are you going to arrest Perry, me, and all the kahunas?" Anne finally asked. She was not mocking him, he understood. She wanted to know how far he would go.

Indeed, the answer interested Tanizaki as well. He, too, wanted to know what it was he held most precious here. The dancers plainly were in a semi-conscious state as they moved. Their gestures were powerful, uninhibited, and completely unlike any "hula" Tanizaki had seen before. "They are possessed by Lakaand Laka's husband, Lono," a kahuna whispered in Japanese in Tanizaki's ear. He shivered. The performers were drugged, he supposed, but appeared to his–admittedly susceptible–eye, to be inhabited by some demonic spirit.

The drums, the chanting, the sound of the nose flute went on and on, for hours perhaps. On and on. Tanizaki watched an impassive David Kalakaua. It could be that the youth was narcotized as well, but his eyes were bright, alert. Kalakaua focused on the ceremony, chanted for a time, then went silent. The singers, the drummers droned interminably.

Tanizaki allowed himself to drowse for a minute or two, untila sudden silence snapped him awake.

Two priests stood at the top of the tower, while one made a dramatic declaration in Polynesian. David Kalakaua marched to the pavilion, clambered onto the wooden platform, and lay prone.

Anne gripped Tanizaki's arm with her fingers, her nails digging deep into his flesh. The others might remain unmoved, bu she could not.

Tanizaki himself stopped breathing and his heart pounded directly into his eardrums. He wanted to shout to the participants to stop, but the carefully created atmosphere held him from doing so. Anne leaned her head against his body and drew at him to comfort her. By the time Tanizaki glanced back, the kahuna had already done his work and the boy was drenched in blood. Other priests dragged away the dead man while Anne murmured words of protest into Tanizaki's chest.

They ate food given first to Pele and the intermittent drumming and chanting continued throughout the remainder of the night.

Tanizaki replayed the scene in his head as dawn lighted their way down the mountainside. What had he seen? Had he witnessed the death of David Kalakaua? Or only a sham? Would the Hawaiians dare make a mockery of their sacred ceremony? And did it, should it, matter to him?

Tanizaki stopped in his tracks and the others halted with him. He drew the boy's confession from his jacket pocket. "What the hell am I supposed to do with this?" he growled and tore the paper into a dozen pieces.

Anne and Perry shifted warily. Not one of the three knew for certain what Tanizaki would do next.

Dressed about as smartly as an officer could be in these islands, where daily necessities were often lacking, Tanizaki strode into the main police station for his 2 p.m. appointment with Baron Shimazo. He had met Shimazo only once before, on his superior's arrival on the Island of Hawaii, but the nobleman was said to be a scholar–to have studied in the West, in fact, at Oxford University in England.

"Deputy Inspector Tanizaki to see Colonel Shimazo," Tanizak declared stiffly to the reception guard as he displayed his identification badge. The guard studied a list of authorized visitors and admitted the detective.

"Ah Takeo-san," Shimazo greeted Tanizaki, who stood crisply at attention until the Baron motioned at him to relax. "Let me give you a drink. I have a bottle of pre-war Scotch. Johnny Walker. The real thing. We're still living off the days of American splendor, aren't we?" Shimazo commented in English. Then he smiled.

Tanizaki was rather taken aback by this pronouncement.

He absolutely had no cache of pre-war whiskey himself. If he was able to scare up the occasional bottle of taro root wine, that was going some. And for Shimazo to refer so casually to the period of American rule...

His superior handed Tanizaki a glass. Ice, too! Tanizaki nodded in acknowledgment, sipped the heady potion with some caution, and waited for Shimazo to go on.

"That fellow you reported as having died on Kilauea? A body was found. My assistant, Detective Sergeant Hiroa, will take you to the morgue to identify it. I think we're all glad that this matter has been concluded. So distressing, really." He smiled urbanely, in a way not at all characteristic of a Japanese officer. "I didn't know Fuchida well, of course. Yet we're all obliged to you for clearing up his murder. That's what our police inspectors are for, aren't they, Takeo? By the way, you don't have a younger brother, Jun, who was at Cambridge, do you? A mathematician?"

Tanizaki's eyebrows crept up ever so slightly. "My cousin," he replied.

"A serious fellow. You didn't yourself study in England?"

"Regrettably, no," muttered Tanizaki. Where in the world was all this leading?

"I do so much admire the Western nations. Time we forgot about the war, isn't it, Inspector? Leave the old ways behind. Get on with the new. There's a lot of potential to the Hawaiian Islands, don't you think? Especially as a tourist spot."

Tanizaki was still puzzling over whether to correct Shimazo's addled reference to his deputy inspector's rank, but before Tanizaki had a chance to speak, Shimazo had picked up the phone and was calling for Hiroa. Tanizaki gulped down the remaining liquor, so as not to waste it. He knew an exit cue when he was being given one.

Hiroa appeared. Tanizaki had finished the Scotch not a moment too soon.

"Show Inspector Tanizaki to the morgue, if you please, Detective Sergeant," Shimazo requested in Japanese.

Tanizaki opened his mouth to assert his proper title.

"No, Takeo. You're an Inspector now. A reward would seem to be appropriate for solving a case this crucial. Case closed, I believe, Inspector. I'm delighted." Police Chief Satoshi Shimazo turned back to his desk.

Almost literally dizzy with the rapidfire dispatch of the interview, Tanizaki followed mechanically a half-step behind Hiroa.

In the morgue, Hiroa slid out a drawer to display the body recovered on Kilauea. "Is this David Kalakaua, the man who confessed to you the murder of Commander Fuchida prior to committing suicide?"

Tanizaki gazed soberly at the body, pulled away the sheet to view...knife wounds. "Yes, Kalakaua, no doubt about it, Detective Sergeant. He killed Commander Fuchida. Of that we can be sure." The wounds, the new Inspector noted, were not, in fact, inconsistent with a report of suicide. Remarkable luck!

Hiroa rolled the dead man back into his temporary niche and saw Tanizaki to the door.

"Congratulations, Inspector, on your promotion," commented Hiroa with some genuine warmth. "I served the Baron in the Marianas the last two years. I think you will find him a capable leader." Hiroa, who had been speaking Japanese for their official business, switched to English for the coda.

"Thank you, Detective Sergeant," Tanizaki replied. "I'm sure we'll meet again soon at the Officers' Club."

"And bring your lovely fiance, Anne Glasgow. The Baron was especially gratified to find you have friends among the Hawaiian ethnics."

The Baron knew a great deal, did he not?

Tanizaki must call Anne as soon as he got back to his own precinct. He hoped she would be pleased to hear of his promotion. Somehow, the way that events had transpired today had cheered him, stirred his natural optimism, which had so recently begun to lag.

Tanizaki had only two questions remaining, but he supposed they were irrelevant.

165

Whose body was it he had just identified so positively as Kalakaua's?

And, who had actually killed Commander Fuchida on the docks?

Be Sure to Wear a Flower in Your Hair

Tanizaki hemmed and hawed as he shifted his weight uncomfortably in the bamboo-and-frond chair opposite his boss's desk. In respect to furniture at least, Commander Shimazo had gone `local.' The seat emitted a creak of protest every time Tanizaki made a move.

He pulled out a tan and yellow handkerchief that flaunted handpainted banyan leaves, and mopped his face. It was no hotter here than usual. Police headquarters on the Big Island was always steaming.

"Just what are you trying to say, Inspector?" prodded Police Commander Satoshi Shimazo.

The problem was twofold. To begin with, Tanizaki loathed having to ask his superior a favor. Secondly, the topic of the boon itself was a risky one.

Still, he had turned the matter over in his mind any number of times and had decided there was no alternative. Moreover, Anne was adamant that Tanizaki do something to help her brother.

"Perry Glasgow," he managed to blurt out after a pause. "My brother-in-law." Even saying those few words was like spilling out a dirty little secret, it brought so much to mind that in the last seven-and-a-half years Tanizaki ought not to have done.

Shimazo continued waiting patiently, an ironic-seeming little smile playing across his face. Bending his head ever-so-slightly, he fiddled with the official seal with which he had been busily stamping police orders when Tanizaki had entered.

"Your lovely wife's brother, yes," agreed Shimazo, placing the signet back in its box and locking it into the top drawer of his desk.

Certainly the Police Commander locked away his seal. Security. Here, among a people who did not welcome its conquerors, every precaution had to be taken. If the Japanese were not vigilant, men like Perry would be on them like lice on a beggar.

"Glasgow's being blackmailed," Tanizaki admitted, his voice descending into a complaint, as if the offense were Perry's, and against Tanizaki personally.

"Ah," exclaimed Shimazo, "a crime!"

Tanizaki never quite understood where he stood with Shimazo, nor what the man's emotions or intentions were. "Yes, sir," he responded as if the conversation were being conducted in all seriousness–as Tanizaki had hoped it might be. "Blackmail *is* a felony."

"Can you arrest the blackmailer?" suggested Shimazo rhetorically, assuming the facsimile of a Commander's concern.

"That wouldn't put Perry in a very good position with the authorities–us, I mean."

"I see," declared Shimazo in mock surprise. "What's he being blackmailed for then? Delaying the mail?" The police chief snickered. The mail in the Islands was so notoriously slow, the Islanders said that letters were still being delivered here describing the bombing of Pearl Harbor. Perry Glasgow ran one of the smaller post offices in Imperial District One.

"It's a political thing," Tanizaki answered sourly.

Shimazo raised his eyebrows. He wasn't overly astonished, that was for sure. But now Shimazo turned quietly somber. Perry was a member of the Hawaiian-Americans League, an active subversive–even terrorist–organization.

Tanizaki wiped his face once more as Shimazo drew his focus into himself. The Police Commander ruminated for quite some time before speaking again. "Might I presume that you are asking me to help Perry Glasgow out of his predicament?"

"Yes, sir, I am." Shimazo was going to put the screws to him. This was not the first such experience for Tanizaki.

"What is it you're going to do for me in return? That's what I really wonder," considered Baron Shimazo.

"Whatever you think would be suitable, sir." In fact,

168

Tanizaki couldn't imagine what it was that Shimazo might have in mind. All the Commander's annoying mannerisms aside, he wasn't venal or a brute. Consequently, the two men almost got along in some respects. Both lived from a sense of rectitude, but both were pragmatists as well.

"I'll have to ask a service of you."

"This is a little bit of blackmail, in itself, isn't it, sir?" Tanizaki couldn't resist pointing that out.

"It's payment, man, that's all it is." Shimazo smiled in a kind of triumph. "I have a couple of errands for you to run. My mother's coming in next Tuesday. I'd like for you to pick her up."

"Yes, sir." Overseas air traffic all landed at Ewa Beach on Oahu.

"Show her around there for the rest of the day. Take her to dinner and so on–on me, of course. Because Wednesday, the Americans are coming in. I'm sure I told you. I'd like you to be their tour guide for the rest of their visit." Shimazo extended his smile into a grin. *Checkmate*, he seemed to be telling Tanizaki. The Police Commander had gotten the dreaded Americans off his back and Tanizaki would have to be the one to stay overnight on Oahu.

The bamboo chair frame groaned yet again under Tanizaki's muscular bulk. Perhaps the sound indicated a restless dissatisfaction on the occupant's part.

"You needn't worry about your brother-in-law," Shimazo promised, clinching the bargain even as he stood, a move that succinctly shooed away the Second Rank Inspector.

Tanizaki dandled his four-month old, Takashi, on his knee. The baby appeared reasonably pleased with his father's regard. The older boys wanted Tanizaki's attention, too, and called out to him every several seconds as they played on the floor with their wax crayons and coloring books. Anne stooped over Tanizaki to reclaim her little one, who thrust his feet into motion in mid-air. *Why do they all do that?* the father wondered.

Eikichi, the eldest, nearly seven years old, had observed

this transaction and shrewdly decided this was the moment to call to his father once more. "Look, papa, I'm drawing a boat. It's the *Killigan III*, Uncle Perry's motor boat."

Perry again! The boys were devoted to their always-joking uncle. "So it is. A perfect representation," the father responded. The paper ocean was a deep and scrawled blue, while the craft itself crested at the top of an enormous swell. A giant aquatic reptile–or was it merely a fish?–swam to starboard. "Very artistic." He adored his boys.

Kulu, age three, competed for dad's acknowledgment of his artwork. "Look, I dwew the beach an' a twee."

Indeed, remarkable as well. Tanizaki's sons were brilliant and ever so talented–or so any fond father would imagine, staring at the lemon-on-white illustration, the brown trunk of a palm curving upward in a true-to-life depiction. Tanizaki praised his second son liberally.

He was charmed by his children–doted on them–and fretted over the prospects for their future. He would like to see them at the university in their home country, Japan, where he himself had gone to school, and where the academics were particularly rigorous. Or at the very least, they must go to England or to Canada–someplace that would prepare them for the remarkable careers that awaited each.

So how was he to provide this on a policeman's salary? Yet if he couldn't give the boys that possibility, the sole other option was a trade school on the Big Island that turned out skilled craftsmen to serve the Imperial territories in the technical fields–such as electronics and medical technology. The only education for the real professionals–architects, engineers, and doctors–was away from here. University training, was thus, based on economics primarily, reserved for the Japanese residing in Japan.

His children by law held his own citizenship. Only prejudice–which continued to exist–and his lack of means could stop them from achieving great things in life.

Kulu came over to sit on Tanizaki's lap. The little boy still liked to be held, and in the last four months since the birth of his young brother, demanded an even greater share of "equal" time than he had before.

Only a handful of Japanese came off the plane–four men and one woman. Straight-backed, slender, and white-haired, there was no doubt that she was an aristocrat. The other passengers were Hawaiians, principally laborers returning home from jobs in Japan. Tanizaki watched the arrivals present their documents to the Entry Control Officer at the gate. As the Baron's mother entered the small, concrete-bunker terminal building, Tanizaki hurried forward and introduced himself.

The Island of Oahu was a no-man's land, unreclaimed since the furious bombings several decades before. Where would the money come from to rebuild, after all? Japan's resources were already stretched thin and nothing would go into a distant, unknown island. Therefore, the military had chosen the relatively untouched Big Island as its headquarters, and had left Oahu to a subculture of impoverishment and crime.

Oahu was rigorously policed by the military, however, with heavily-armed three-man teams roaming together to provide strength in numbers. Their aim was not so much to protect Hawaiian from Hawaiian–why should the Japanese care–but to make sure that, in the end, Imperial forces still held the upper hand.

Hold this country? What was the purpose, if Japan chose to invest nothing into bettering the place? Hawaii was still the doorway between the Pacific and the United States, and to a nation for which a defensive stance against the remainder of the world was a reflex, the importance of retaining possession of this dreadful land was obvious.

Tanizaki and the Baron's mother, Miako Shimazo, registered at the one spot on Oahu a Japanese could feel safe–the guesthouse within the naval compound, a less than charming overnight retreat despite a strenuous effort to provide all the luxuries. The armed service is the armed service and this was hardly a vacation spot.

Tanizaki fell all over himself apologizing to the Police Commander's mother. He wasn't trying to make up to her for any reason, he simply felt it was wrong for the genteel woman to experience a place like this. He was absolutely furious at Shimazo.

"That's my son. I might have expected it. A typical male," she told her escort in an offhand reply. "No thought in his mind except for his work. Never mind, Takeo. I'm nearly 80 years old. I'm long past needing to be entertained. I'm glad that we can have a quiet dinner together, anyway, and talk. You can tell me about yourself. Then tomorrow, I will see my child."

Good grief, to think of it that way, that the Police Commander was this woman's offspring, that he had been a baby, just like Tanizaki's own Takashi. Some father had powdered him and soothed his cries, even as Tanizaki did with his own sons. Such a scenario stood out as more impossible than possible.

The Americans arrived in a small private plane from someplace they kept referring to as "the Coast." Other than suspecting that "the Coast" was on the Pacific seacoast of North America, Tanizaki wasn't sure where it was they meant. The three of them, including the woman, cozily wrung the hand of the Baroness Shimazo, an act that filled Tanizaki with great horror and shame. Good heavens! Their fingers must be teeming with all sorts of germs, coming from wherever they had come from. And they spoke so loudly, with such enthusiasm—like children, really.

The Baroness was completely gracious with these terrible foreigners and Tanizaki was greatly impressed by her demeanor. But he longed to keep her away from them and shielded her at every opportunity. Soon, however, the group passed through the Military Control Station at Waikiki and stepped onto the ferry that would take them back to the Big Island.

The American in authority, Al Howard (which was the first name and which was the last?), stood so near to Tanizaki at the ship's rail that the Inspector was forced to move away to distance himself. Why did these people want to be so close?

Tanizaki was acquainted with "Americans," naturally, but Hawaiian-Americans, a subject people in a sense, most of whom would not risk being too brash with their Japanese governors. *Those* Americans had learned tamer manners over the years and, in fact, now satisfactorily reflected the Japanese mode of behavior, so that they were comfortable to be around.

Why, Tanizaki had even married an American. She was part Polynesian though, and wasn't truly all that well-behaved. Anne had a cutting edge, but most of the time she kept it sheathed–not that Tanizaki didn't occasionally enjoy a flash of steel.

"It's very exciting for us to be here," said Howard (Al?). "Now that an updated Japanese-U.S. trade agreement has finally been approved, my company feels there is a great deal of business to be done in Hawaii. You can expect a flood of money guys like us, in suits, any time now."

Tanizaki, as usual, wore a shortsleeved and lightweight uniform, proper to the climate. "Business is not an interest of mine," he retorted sourly, staring toward the looming land mass that approached. The Island of Hawaii revealed itself like a familiar lover, verdant in long, lush stretches, starkly-naked rock from other views. "I'm a policeman."

"Even a cop is interested in profit," Howard rejoined in a flash, beaming broadly.

"Cop?" Tanizaki had already discerned that these people had a peculiarly colloquial vocabulary. Their English was not quite the English that he spoke.

"I thought we were going to be driven around Oahu today. That's the island that was the most popular for tourism in the 1930s."

"That's where Pearl Harbor was," Tanizaki answered, by way of explanation.

"Yes, the big Navy base yielded a lot of dollars for restaurants and hotels."

"The area was decimated," Tanizaki told the man with

satisfaction, as if the bombings were a step he singlehandedly had undertaken against this Howard. "The structures that weren't damaged in the initial assault were mostly leveled when the Japanese forces came on shore. There was house-to-house fighting for a while. The hotels were torn down afterward so they wouldn't serve as centers of resistance." Although Tanizaki was a policeman and not a military tactician, he nodded happily to himself at the wisdom of that strategy.

Howard stared at Tanizaki, but without hostility. "There should be a lot of free beachfront property then."

"Occupied by gun installations mostly," Tanizaki commented.

"Picturesque?" asked Howard.

Perhaps the two of them hadn't quite the same idea as to what `picturesque' meant. Could rocket launchers pointed toward the sea and sailors routinely peering through telescopes to check for enemy warships be considered a sight of some aesthetic appeal? Tanizaki cast a baffled glance at Howard.

"Here's what I'm getting at," said the businessman. "I don't know you, but you seem to be a guy with a head on his shoulders. You're a smart fellow, out for a buck like the rest of us. I mean, out for a yen." He showed his teeth. "The Hawaiian Islands are going to be a tourist spot again soon enough. It's part-and-parcel of the future. There's a lot of money to be made in real estate. One of my objectives on this trip is to obtain a few pieces of desirable land—as much as I can negotiate for, to tell you the truth—although I am inclined to hedge a bit on the site. Some acreage on Oahu and a couple of lots on the Island of Hawaii. Depending on our gut instincts, of course."

The idea had never been to allow these people to set up shop locally. The Japanese government hoped in opening itself to commerce with the United States that this would promote a strong Hawaiian export business. Such was the main intention, anyway. Selling to the U.S. would bring American wealth into Hawaii.

"The property here is owned by Japanese nationals, and

by some natives under license from the administration," Tanizaki informed Howard stiffly. "That's the law."

"I know that," agreed Howard with a nod. "Which is why we'll be looking for a smart business partner. Someone qualified to own the land without encumbrance. A Japanese citizen, in other words. He's the one who'd have his name on any contract. He'd be the figurehead–it would be our money behind it and we'd run the corporation. The Japanese associate wouldn't have to do any actual work, you see. But he'd get, say, a percentage of the purchase price, and other eventual royalties. First, we'd negotiate and spell it all out. We have extensive resources to pour into Hawaii and we anticipate the possibility of later expansion on this base."

Tanizaki frowned, pondering what he had been so bluntly told. "That sounds fraudulent to me," he evaluated. He glared at Howard. "It's all a matter of intent. The intent would obviously be to commit a fraud."

"Mother told me about your talk!" The Police Commander was passing Tanizaki in the hall at headquarters. Generally, deep in conversation with someone of greater importance than Tanizaki, Shimazo wouldn't volunteer to speak to his subordinate at such an instance.

Tanizaki stopped in his tracks after his chief did. "Your mother's a very charming woman," he observed. The Baroness was like a faded rose–reminiscent of a beauty once sublime, still promising a pleasing scent, though one transformed from its original perfume and appealing to a different caliber of appreciation.

Shimazo was gratified. "You'll have to come to dinner. On Friday night, perhaps. I'll let you know." The Commander began walking off again on some pressing errand or other. Friday night, if Shimazo had asked, was pretty much reserved for outings with the kids.

"Bring your family, too." The Commander had raised his voice so that Tanizaki could hear him from further away. So could everyone else transversing the hall. "Mother is very eager to meet them."

Tanizaki turned red as if he had been caught trying to curry favor with the chief. He despised that sort of thing, which was probably why he had gotten no further than he had–and at such a remote station. But whenever that thought went through his mind, Tanizaki remembered: Because he was here, he had met Anne, and the rest had followed. It was like a miracle, really. He had not ever considered himself a very likely candidate for the married life. And yet, how sad if he had missed such joys. He would never have known exactly what was absent from his life. A part of him would never have been born.

The most annoying aspect of the chief's invitation was that Tanizaki had resolved to stay away from Shimazo for a while–to be more distant. He had decided, despite his better judgment and an innate impulse to live a strictly ethical life no matter the cost, to propose himself as the front man for the American syndicate. How he disliked these people–their manners principally, or lack of them! But here was a way he could assure his children's prospects.

Any money he made would go into an account abroad for their education. The funds would be safe–even if Tanizaki himself were eventually caught. He had to face up to that possibility! As a policeman, he had seen that most criminals never imagined they could be apprehended. Still, so many were. If he should be confronted with his own complicity in this fraud, that would not be so bad. It would only be serious if he were brought to trial. That, however, was fairly unlikely. The authorities would not want to try a Japanese national in the Islands for a mere act of financial deception–however illegal on the surface of it. Tanizaki, despite all within him that balked at his moral comedown in the world, would volunteer to take that chance.

There was another reason why Tanizaki wished to separate himself from Police Commander Shimazo Satoshi. During the long dinner conversation he had engaged in with the Baroness, she had apparently discovered some connection between her family and Tanizaki's. Such a link between the Baron's family and his was annoying, to say the least, and Tanizaki wished to disassociate himself from it.

Tanizaki's grandfather, or so the Baroness said, had been the steward at the Shimazo estates–a long-time and valued retainer, she claimed. Tanizaki didn't like the sound of that. He pictured a leathery old man snipping at the rose bushes, gathering blooms for the Shimazo Family table. This was not an image of his antecedents that Tanizaki wished to hold, nor was it the role he desired to take in his relationship with the chief.

Proud and willful though Inspector Tanizaki was, he appeared as bidden at the Baron's bungalow on Friday night, wife and little ones in tow. Since the Baron couldn't have meant for them to bring the baby, Uncle Perry was staying with Takashi. This, as usual, irked Tanizaki's sense of propriety, especially now with the blackmail issue and Perry's Hawaiian-Americans connection up in the air.

The Baroness grabbed onto Eikichi and Kulu as if they were her own grandchildren, fussing over them in what Tanizaki considered to be an excessive manner. They were engaging, well-mannered, and darling children, it was true, but they were not part of the Baroness's blood line.

Actual tears, however, came to the Baroness's eyes, which shined with great emotion. "You don't realize what your grandmother was to me, you see," she told Tanizaki using her stiff but surprisingly flawless English for Anne's benefit. "She was my best friend–my only friend, really–for many years. She was a wonderful, remarkable woman. I cared so much for her."

Tanizaki remembered his grandmother somewhat, although that recollection was a distant one. She had given him a yellow- and black-striped toy tiger with a tail that twirled. He had been fond of her, and fascinated by the difference in her features from those of most of the people around him. But she had died when he was about six and his father had died early on as well.

"My mother is much happier to see you than me on this trip," observed the Baron with a cheerful laugh. He was obviously secure enough in his mother's love that he had no sense of jealousy. Tanizaki had never observed Shimazo being snappish, come to think of it, except when it came to matters under his official purview.

The Inspector would have preferred dropping the entire subject of ancestors, but the Baroness was intent upon it. Throughout the dinner—quite a bit more elegant than any that Tanizaki and his wife enjoyed at home—the frost-haired woman kept up the talk not only of Grandmother Miriam, but of "the old days," and the current Baron's father and grandparents.

The Baron ate his roast pig a bit too enthusiastically, and beamed a droll expression out toward Tanizaki. Anne probably didn't notice, since she was much too busy interrogating the Baroness as the stories unfurled. The boys got bored with the adults' talk, talk, talk and Shimazo had one of his Polynesian maids take them out to see the fish pond in back. Tanizaki would have followed to make doubly sure that the boys didn't fall in—and to get away from the chatter, as well—but the Baron stopped him. "Wait a minute," he requested in a tone of command that grated on Tanizaki in the persona of dinner guest.

The Baron rinsed his fingers in a bowl of warm water and lemon slice. He rose while drying his hands, then indicated for his subordinate to follow him. This need for privacy to say whatever seemed to be on Shimazo's mind aroused Tanizaki's curiosity. His instincts were alerted to the possibility of police business.

The two men stepped into the Police Commander's den off the patio. The sliding glass door was open and a cool evening breeze streamed in. Since this enclave was reserved exclusively for Japanese nationals, security was relatively tight up here. An open door was not as foolish as it seemed, considering that of 27 murders on the Island last year—not a lot for the total population, honestly—a disproportionate number—17—had been of the ruling hierarchy.

Tanizaki sat on Shimazo's green leather sofa. Green leather! Good heavens! Where had this come from? An antique from the days of American rule, most likely. The Police Commander led the good life. A stab of anger surged up in Tanizaki. Perhaps here was some justification for throwing in his lot with the Americans.

Shimazo lit a cigar and poured himself and Tanizaki each a brandy. "I wanted to let you know what I've done about Perry."

This was not a conversation to which Tanizaki had looked forward.

The Police Commander cracked a smile. "Nothing to draw attention to your brother-in-law. No. I've rehabilitated the whole Hawaiian-American pack instead. I've signed a declaration to that effect."

Tanizaki was taken utterly by surprise. He thought about the implications. The Hawaiian-Americans League was no "namby-pamby" group, as Perry would say. It was well-organized and had perpetrated at least one assassination to Tanizaki's knowledge.

"Since it's not an outlaw association any longer, Perry Glasgow can't be blackmailed." The Police Commander sat back easily in his padded swivel chair—another pre-war relic, no doubt.

Tanizaki hesitated. He could hardly ask his superior whether such an action was truly wise.

Shimazo leaned forward again, as if to impart some awesome revelation to the man opposite. "I think it's a greater mistake to drive a group like that further underground, don't you? Let's get them out in the open, so everyone knows exactly who they are. A circle of old men, who are never going to do anything, for the most part. They're no heros. In fact, if you speak to Sasai, who's heading anti-terrorism now, these men are has-beens. We already know who most of them are anyway, of course. Now let the Islanders find out who they are, too. If the League wants to recruit, frankly, it's fine with us. Newer, less committed members will only dilute the organization, pull it down."

That was one theory, one possibility. Tanizaki's training had been in police procedures and crime, not in politics, but he saw several holes in the Baron's reasoning.

Shimazo perceived that he wasn't getting through to Tanizaki. "Subversive? Well, I guess. But there are other threats." Shimazo spoke passionately. "You've heard of the Fusion Party, I suppose."

Tanizaki nodded, but he quite couldn't connect what he had heard about them with the word "threat." The Fusioneers, as the group sometimes called itself, was only a band of kids–boys and girls in their teens and early 20s. Their philosophy sounded innocent enough to Tanizaki, They believed in harmony between the Hawaiian ethnicities and the Japanese in their midst. Tanizaki thought this was a hopeful sign that the next generation would accept Japanese rule and that the two cultures would blend peacefully.

"Here's a paper Sasai brought me the other day. These are the lyrics to a song of theirs, actually." Shimazo passed a flyer to Tanizaki.

Fusion, No Confusion
People! Do you know just who you are?
Polynesian, Amer-i-can,
Japanese, Chinese.
Hawaiian Islanders all.
It's no invasion. It's simply Asian.
The conquered are the conquerors.
Aloha Oe. Aloha Oe.
Welcome to our happy land.
We wan' fusion, forget about confusion.
Pro-fusion is the way to go....

Tanizaki read it and laughed. "Their meter is a little off." He smiled benignly.

"*The conquered are the conquerors?*" the Police

Commander emphasized.

Tanizaki continued to wear a smile on his face. Was he an utter fool? he wondered. He was one of those warriors who had been overwhelmed by fusion. His family was Hawaiian, and he was about to deal with the Americans against the interests of the Japanese. Furthermore, he knew full well that he would never live in Japan again. He was the prime example of a Japanese who had been completely fused.

The air blowing in from the ocean was thick with humidity and Tanizaki dripped with either sweat or condensation. The sand had been invaded by a gaggle of youngsters setting up for a school-less day. A boy strummed his ukulele.

Once again, Tanizaki was trooping the Americans all over the Island. "We had our hearts set on Oahu," nagged the woman, Melissa Goldman, whose name reminded Tanizaki of his own grandmother, Miriam. "Will we get to see it on the way back?"

"There really isn't anything there," replied Tanizaki doubtfully. "Only..." he searched for the proper English word... "squalor."

"That's okay," Melissa replied. "That doesn't matter. We want to create an encapsulated resort. So long as the beaches are beautiful, the rest doesn't matter. Or, it does, but we'll build up the whole Island, eventually." Her eyes smiled at him, in such a way... If he cheated on Anne, she would either leave him or kill him, he wasn't sure which—especially now that she had just had their third child and was dangerously unsure of her attractiveness to him.

"I'll take you to the beach at Kaimu." His response was stiff. Kaimu was fairly private. He looked around to see where their car and driver were. All this gasoline just to tote these foreigners around! If they were going to put Americans somewhere on the Island, that might be a good spot.

"What about that property we saw up on the cliffs before?" asked Howard. "The views were remarkable."

"That's the Japanese residential district," Tanizaki answered in horror. Good grief. These people!

"Oh, I see. Nice spot for a honeymooners' colony." Howard's look was a calculating one. "Just kidding, of course."

"No beach," Melissa reminded her boss.

"An elevator down to the shore might work..."

Tanizaki finally made out the words the Polynesian boy was singing. No surprise, really: "*It's no invasion, it's simply Asian.*" Darn those children. After taking the Hawaiian-Americans off the outlawed list, Shimazo had declared the Fusion Party to be illegal. Was Tanizaki supposed to arrest these babies? That made no sense.

"I'll see if I can take you over to one of the other islands tomorrow," Tanizaki promised. Shimazo wouldn't like having his home sold off for newly marrieds, would he now?

Howard slapped Tanizaki on the back, but the policeman didn't jump in alarm as he had the first time. He was almost getting used to it..

A Polynesian girl, plump in orange shorts, had come over to distribute vanda orchids to each of them. "Welcome to our happy land," she told them in total, doe-eyed sincerity.

"I'm one of the owners of your happy land," Tanizaki grumbled at her provocatively.

"We love you all," she said. "Aloha oe."

Tanizaki was parched and looked forward to stepping into the house and pouring himself a cold lemonade. After they had inspected property the entire morning, Howard had suggested that the "gang" stop for some "pizza" and a beer. Tanizaki wasn't sure just what pizza was, to the great amazement of Howard, Ron, and Melissa. They couldn't understand a culture that did not serve this specific food. From their description, pizza was something like a big pancake with tomato sauce. Ugh! And as for the beer, hadn't they realized yet that alcoholic beverages weren't served in public—except in some on the Japanese private clubs? He didn't understand that they didn't understand that either; there were such tremendous implications for public safety.

At last Tanizaki had dropped them off at their guest bungalow. (How did they arrange it with two men and one woman, anyway?) He had settled it with Howard. Tanizaki would be their "front man" for whatever amount it was that Howard had specified. Strangely, considering he was doing this for the money, Tanizaki hadn't paid very close attention to that part of the transaction. He had felt too ashamed.

It was now also obvious to him that he was going to get caught. He knew he would. There was no way he could cover over something this big. What had he been thinking of, anyway? Nevertheless, he was going ahead with the deal... *Was he so self-destructive then? What point was he trying to make?*

Tanizaki had spent the rest of the afternoon at the tiny Real Estate Registration Office in police headquarters. How obvious could you get? He had sat there for two hours or more, asking the clerk for record after record. Was she not supposed to remember him during a subsequent investigation?

Still, his research was tremendously enlightening. He had been very vague as to the ownership of most of the property in the Islands. He now knew that 90 percent of the volcanic ash under their feet–for such was the composition of the dry "earth"–belonged, in fact, to Moritomo Industries, a Japanese import/export and technologies firm. Other large tracts of land were simply owned by the Japanese government, while an acre here and there "belonged" to one of the very few rich Hawaiians licensed by the Japanese as landowners. This was all quite a peculiar set-up, one that Tanizaki didn't comprehend very well. From what he saw though, Imperial Japan had seized ownership when the Islands had been occupied; thereafter, beginning about seven or eight years ago, the government had sold off lots to Moritomo.

Most of the land the Americans now wanted to buy, and for which Tanizaki was to negotiate, was registered to this Japanese corporate entity. All that Tanizaki could find on the documents, however, was the Police Commander's official stamp. On not one single page was there the name of a local representative for Moritomo.

Inside Tanizaki's house, the fans rotated full speed and the rooms were almost a bearable temperature. Although the Tanizakis lived in a Japanese neighborhood, the area was nowhere near so exclusive as the enclave in which Shimazo's home stood. Protection in this district was frighteningly slender and Tanizaki had installed bars on all the windows. He hated the sight of them.

He heard conversation coming from the patio and, anticipating his children's joyful reception, walked out there with a glass in his hand. The boys were absorbed in the blandishments of their visitor–Baroness Shimazo. She had Kulu's face in her hand and she was telling the children what precious darlings they were. Tanizaki was tempted for a moment to be jealous of the boys' attentiveness to the Baroness, but it was difficult to begrudge the 78-year-old woman anything. She was also leaving the Islands in a few more days.

This congenial group turned around to look as Tanizaki infringed upon the scene. Anne gave her husband a special smile that struck him to the heart. He wasn't going to carry out that pact with the Americans, and that was final! The boys could become fishermen, if it came to that. He wouldn't leave Anne here on her own while he went to prison in Japan. He was hard-headed and devious, but he wasn't cut out for a life, or even a portion of a life, of crime.

"They're beautiful children, Takeo," the Baroness addressed him. "How Miriam would have loved to have seen the three of them." She turned to the boys. "She was a remarkable woman, your great-grandmother–a very unusual woman for her day."

Tanizaki sat down, taking the baby from Anne and placing him on his own lap.

"Yes," said the Baroness, watching Takashi. "Yes, I can see the resemblance." She gazed brightly at Tanizaki, with tears in her eyes.

"Does he look like my grandmother?" asked the policeman in bewilderment, searching the baby's face for what he remembered of his grandmother's features.

"No," said the Baroness. "Not like Miriam. No, he looks exactly like his great-grandfather." She glanced at the older children, to see if they were listening. "Like the Baron," she whispered. "Shimazo Noburu was your father's real father."

"I've sold half the Oahu beachfront to the Americans." Perry said in Polynesian to his sister Anne.

Tanizaki had just brought the palm wine in from the kitchen when he heard this remark. A cold fury socked Tanizaki in the chest. After seven years in the Islands, he could understand pidgin Hawaiian well enough. What mischief was his brother-in-law up to now? He himself had given up any profit to be made from the Americans. Had Perry found a way to take the money for himself? ...And just how was Tanizaki going to have to lower himself to get Perry out of this mess?

"You've done what?" he demanded.

"Ah ha, the policeman," Perry said. "It's a joke of course. I'm just joking."

"You can't have sold the Oahu beachfront because it's owned by Moritomo Industries."

"That's true," agreed Perry. "But who is Moritomo? And what if I have a property transfer and licensing certificate, all signed and properly stamped?"

"Shimazo isn't anyone you can pay off," Tanizaki informed Perry. "And he's the man with the seal."

"You're right again, of course," Perry acknowledged. "I'm really not going to do anything like that. Just speaking off the top of my head."

"That's good," Anne interjected coldly. "It's one thing to take action for our independence." She paused to glare at her husband in accusation of all the wrongs committed by the Japanese against her people. "It's another matter entirely to commit crimes out of personal greed." This time she delivered a censorious look straight at her brother.

Both men appeared properly chagrined, and no more was mentioned of the matter.

Which didn't mean that Tanizaki had stopped thinking of it. Nothing good was going to come of the Americans' visit and he wished they'd leave and never come back—no, not any of them. Island politics was complicated enough already. And that Melissa continued to flirt with him, which was entirely disconcerting. But perhaps her doing so was calculated. Even if he wasn't going to be their "front man," there was something the Americans wanted from him—if only silence as to their improper intentions.

Tanizaki reported in to the Police Commander later that week. He quickly reviewed a few of the more significant cases he was working on—a house robbery and an assault. He mentioned taking the Americans up to Kihola Bay, then paused uneasily. Shimazo really wasn't paying very much attention. He continued processing documents as Tanizaki spoke.

"I was wondering, too..."

Shimazo grunted.

"Moritomo Industries. Have you heard the name?"

The Baron looked up at length—in puzzlement. "Big Japanese conglomerate. Don't you know them?" His eyes were two searchlights, totally concentrated on Tanizaki.

"I came across them in conjunction with some Hawaiian land deals," Tanizaki admitted reluctantly. He felt relieved at not having put himself at risk over an arrangement with the Americans. He would have been no good at that!

Shimazo smiled and bent back over his paperwork. "Moritomo is a company owned by my mother, essentially. I've bought some land from the government for Moritomo since I've been here. I mean, she's a principle stockholder in the corporation. She owns about 60 percent—due entirely, she says, to your grandmother's foresight."

His grandmother and the Shimazos again! Tanizaki didn't care to hear anymore. He didn't want information about his grandmother as the concubine to the old Baron. The topic was distasteful to him, as was the concept that the Police Commander might be his own cousin! Well, actually, he felt guilty about that. Somehow he believed in family loyalty. He didn't want to think that he owed Shimazo anything. That would take away a fragment of his independence. Of course any freedom of choice he thought he had about anything, was probably quite imaginary anyway!

Shimazo glanced up again at Tanizaki and laughed. "My mother's wealthy as heck, although you can't tell it by her lifestyle. And you couldn't tell it by me, either. I'm a samurai, after all. We don't care for those things, do we Takeo?" He forcefully stamped a few more papers.

Tanizaki didn't venture to answer that one. Shimazo lived quite well on his salary, due to his position. Tanizaki, on the other hand, had a family to support on considerably less than Shimazo's annual pay. He wondered how Eikichi was going to tolerate the fisherman's life, to which his father had so cavalierly assigned him. The child had gotten seasick the last time they'd gone out on a boat. So much for the genes of a South Sea Islander.

Because Tanizaki was still worried about Perry's comment to Anne–that he was selling Oahu beachfront to the Americans–Tanizaki showed up at Perry's post office the next afternoon. Perry, a postmaster now, was in his office with his feet up on the desk. He was reading an American magazine about hog farming. "I have to make some real money," Perry said. "This job is driving me crazy."

"Maybe if you did some actual work, it wouldn't upset you so much." Tanizaki pointed out.

Perry looked interested. "Is there something bothering you?" he asked. He put down the colorful and dreadfully repulsive pictures of hog snouts and degenerative hog ailments. The photograph on the cover of the publication was that of an animal proudly wearing a blue ribbon that said "First Prize." Or, really, did the animal look proud and coy as the pose would suggest? By now the pig was undoubtedly dead anyway–served with sauce at a barbecue.

"Are you fucking around with the Americans?" Tanizaki demanded. He had learned a great deal of useful English since he had come to the Islands.

"I did offer to sell them some land on Oahu," Perry admitted. He shrugged. "They told me they'd feel more secure if they bought it from a Japanese. They know it's hard for a native to get a license."

Tanizaki felt relieved. He didn't need any more trouble over Perry. He chuckled and rose from the postmaster's visitor's chair. "All right," he said with a certain expansiveness.

Perry stopped his brother-in-law with a gesture. "Sit down. I have to tell you something." The usually carefree Perry actually looked troubled.

Though inclined to depart immediately, Tanizaki sat.

"It's about your boss," Perry continued. "He did me a favor. Really, he acted rather broad-mindedly, I think. I can't decide exactly what he was counting on, but legalizing the Hawaiian-Americans is the best thing he could have done for us. It's better if we're an open organization. This way we're able to show respect for our roots, for the old Polynesian customs and religion. Which is the point." He took his feet down from the desktop while delivering this speech. "I figure I owe him something. And you like Shimazo, too, I suppose. You probably feel a certain amount of loyalty to him."

Tanizaki considered the fact that Shimazo might be his father's own nephew. "I... Yes. I... Well, yes."

Perry nodded in agreement. Such feelings were certainly not easy ones to express. "Not everyone is happy with him," Perry added softly. His eyes were directed out the window. There was nothing out there–palm trees, hibiscus and bougainvillea bushes, cloudless blue sky. "Sometimes men are killed in back alleys or their cars are stopped as they are driving home."

Perry was referring to two recent unsolved murders in particular–both of Japanese nationals. Tanizaki turned red with a sudden rush of conflicting emotions. He wanted to hoist Perry from his chair and fling him up against the wall, demanding to know who the killers were. He was also grateful for the alert about Shimazo. As he very consciously, deliberately, and with great effort, held himself still, he realized how much the warning, and the revelation about the murders, had cost Anne's brother. This was a kind of collaboration with the Japanese against his own. He had set himself in opposition to the terrorist league of which he was himself a member.

The flyers were pasted onto the outside of headquarters, a building occupied 24-hours a day by the Imperial Police.

This Land Is Free
Boys and girls. Mothers and fathers.
This land is free. Our land is free.
No one can contain it, or put it in a bottle.
They cannot scoop it up and take it home.
The land goes or stays where It wants to.
This land is free. It belongs to itself.
Can't put it in a hat; can't place it in a suitcase.
It can't be owned.
Police Commander Shimazo, General Takahashi, you can seize
the sand in your shoes. Other than that, we' ll give you a shovel
so you can ship our homeland to your home.
If you can do that, it won't be Hawaii.
Hawaii will still be here in our hearts.

Officers of the law were trying to efface these noble words by wetting down the blue-colored paper and scraping it off the walls with razor-edged metal tools. Shimazo steamed up to Tanizaki as he was reading a flyer that had not yet been attacked by this janitorial brigade. "Look at that," he said, as if Tanizaki weren't. "It's the work of the Fusion Party. Now you see that I was justified in outlawing the group."

"Could be someone else," Tanizaki objected. "Could be some other organization. Even the Hawaiian-Americans League."

"And that–did you notice that?" Shimazo plunked a fingertip onto a spot on the poster where the final outrage lay. Affixed to this rather meager example of the Poet's art was the stamp of authority, the signet of the Police Commander himself, Baron Shimazo. Shimazo shook his head in complete amazement and exasperation. "My stamp. They stole my stamp!"

"They might have made up one of their own. Yours can't be missing, can it?"

"It's not there! I just checked. Can you imagine–one of them has dared to walk into the police station and take my stamp–from a locked drawer." Shimazo was incredulous.

Tanizaki offered a grimace of sympathy. "Terrible," he muttered. "But really, it's a child's prank."

"Don't you see though," refuted Shimazo excitedly. "This kind of thing undermines our authority."

"It's a shame, sir, absolutely," acknowledged Tanizaki, "but perhaps it makes us look more foolish if we make too big a fuss over it."

Shimazo took a moment to urge his men to remove the flyers a little bit faster–before they were read by the general public. "Our counter-terrorism chief Sasai has found out their meeting place. They gather and stay over in a hut by the beach at Papaaloa. I've planned a raid at 0600, tomorrow morning. I'll want you there."

"Yes, sir," Tanizaki agreed automatically, wondering what time he would have to wake up to join Shimazo in this ludicrous expedition.

"We'll meet here first at 0400," Shimazo snapped. "I'll lay out my plans for everyone at that time."

As Tanizaki began to reflect on what Anne would say when he got out of bed a little after three, a sergeant in the Street Patrol Division ran up. "Sir," he shouted, unexpectedly saluting, military style. "Posters–these posters, sir–they're everywhere–outside of all the stores on Tojo Street at Tokyo Square." The man's eyes were wild at the thought of this breach of the Imperial peace. "I don't know how we're going to get them all down."

Shimazo groaned, as if he had been struck. "I'll call General Takahashi," he cried, suddenly inspired. "We'll get out the regiment."

The Police Commander disappeared without even a signal to Tanizaki, who was mumbling how the Japanese were all going to look like blockheads.

The raiding party had formed up at exactly 4 a.m. Tanizaki, wearing a helmet, was in the position of having to give orders for the sort of maneuver he had ceased participating in years ago. He practiced thumping his hand with the riot stick he had been issued. Did Shimazo imagine his officers were going to wade in and club a bunch of adolescents? Did Shimazo think their parents were so cowed by the Japanese rulers that they would stand for it?

Tanizaki didn't believe that the chief had the stomach for extensive carnage. But from the start, the man hadn't been thinking rationally on the topic of the Fusion Party. He actually saw the Hawaiian-Americans League as less of a danger. He saw them as a crew of old fogies harkening back to the glory days of American dominance, a time of free-flowing American cash. The worrisome thing about the Fusion kids, in Shimazo's view, was that they were trying to imitate the outrageously rebellious style of the American youth of today.

Although all foreign influences had been forbidden in the Islands for the last 50 years, cultural artifacts had a way of creeping in. American magazines showed up and were even passed around in the lunchroom at police headquarters. The Islanders all had broadband radios that picked up programs beamed at them by Radio Free Hawaii. Obviously the Japanese tried to jam the signal, but the success of that often depended on forces of nature outside their control.

Tanizaki was sure that the Hawaiians as a whole had gone to bed last night sniggering about the Japanese haste to clean up the juvenile posters spread all over town. Well, at least the Hawaiians had gone to sleep with a good laugh–and were getting more rest than the Japanese on duty this morning had.

Thirty Japanese policeman, dressed to kill so to speak, were now loading themselves into a single rickety police bus that had once taken Hawaiian children to elementary school. It was a matter of grave concern to the Imperial government that these little ones devotedly study such subjects as the Japanese language and Japanese geography. Something about that struck Tanizaki as absurd.

He closed his eyes and tried to relax. But Shimazo clambered in beside him and began whispering into his ear, nervously running over the plans for their unexpected assault on a troupe of milk-scented native preteens. Tanizaki kept his eyes shut and vocalized fragmentary sounds in acknowledgment every couple of seconds. A few minutes later, he began to doze. In a short while, the bus stopped, shaking him awake.

At first he thought the vehicle had broken down–which wouldn't have been entirely astounding. But no, he had slept longer than he'd imagined. They'd arrived. The Japanese officers began forming in attack squads in the dark, fifty yards down the beach from a tumbledown shack that didn't look big enough to house more than five to seven teenagers at the same time. Five to seven? Maybe it was more like six to eight. Tanizaki supposed this was a place that the kids brought their "dates." Unless the young Hawaiians wanted to listen to lectures on Haiku or practice their flower arranging, there wasn't a great deal for them to do on the Big Island.

Shimazo was ecstatic, Tanizaki noted. The man's ancestors had been great warriors, after all. Damn, *his* ancestors, as well! So why did he feel nothing but disdain for this military-style exercise?

Tanizaki was in the advance detail while Shimazo stayed

192

behind to direct the operation. Sure, what if the kids had guns? Not likely though. The Japanese military and police command had exerted that much control over the last few decades.

The officers crept forward, face masks on. Tear gas was the weapon of choice and Onishi, recently arrived from home, claimed to have good aim. How accurate did one's pitching have to be, however, when tossing a device into a 12- by 15-foot "outhouse," in an area with no other structures?

A risk existed that the CS gas would prove to be an incendiary. Wasn't the Police Commander the slightest bit afraid that the building would catch fire, burning to death the young people inside? Tanizaki felt a twinge or two of annoyance. *We wan' fusion, forget about confusion.*

He heard the click of a rifle being readied for the charge. "For heaven's sake, no shooting," he whispered a little too loudly. "We don't want to wind up firing on ourselves." The men were tense, ready to make their move. Tanizaki wasn't sure whether they were paying any attention to him. As another squad shuffled up behind them in the dark, the Inspector felt a major impulse to hit the deck. If all these policemen were going to start discharging their weapons, he wanted to be someplace else. Like home in bed and hearing about this whole thing afterward.

They were waiting for him to give the signal, but Tanizaki had been lost in thought. Shimazo crept forward to crouch beside him. "Go ahead, get them going," he ordered the Inspector. "What are you waiting for?" At Shimazo's command, Onishi lobbed the gas grenade into the building.

Counting to 10, Tanizaki gave his men a sharp wave of the hand, releasing them from their passivity and swinging them into action.

Fifteen officers flattened the rickety door and burst into the shack, practically crashing through the wall opposite, the space was so narrow. Tanizaki almost guffawed at the idiocy of the situation. The second line of troopers hurried up after them, bayonets fixed. Tanizaki took one look into the room and backed away from the little house. Behind the mask intended to protect him from the fumes, his face had stretched into a smile. He tried to restrain the laughter that bubbled up inside, but the force of his emotion knocked him down onto the sand. The face piece pressed against him and he had to tear it off, his hilarity was choking him so.

The courageous law enforcers who had entered the teens' otherwise empty hangout had come upon a ceiling full of colorful birthday balloons and toilet paper streamers. A sign on each of the walls exuberantly proclaimed, "Aloha Oe. Welcome to our happy home."

Although only Japanese nationals had been present at the ill-fated event, it was completely impossible to keep what had occurred under wraps. How did these rumors spread? Maybe one of the officers had told his Polynesian mistress–and from there on any secrecy was lost. If Shimazo had been considered a buffoon the day before, today the entire Island was pointing directly at him as he passed, and taking considerable delight in the cleverness of their youngsters.

Shimazo admitted sadly to Tanizaki that perhaps his actions had been a bit precipitous–perhaps he had lost his temper too easily and should have seen the posters more as a joke. He shrugged his shoulders helplessly. "Kids," he finally agreed with Tanizaki. "Never having been a father, I couldn't guess how to handle them..." He looked to Tanizaki for some support, which didn't seem to be forthcoming.

"Tokyo has transferred me back home," Shimazo added glumly. "I'm on the flight tomorrow with mother," he continued. "I've only told her that I want to accompany her back to Japan and spend some time with her there."

"I'm sure she'll appreciate it." Tanizaki at last gave his encouragement.

"I shall return," insisted the Police Commander gruffly.

"It's all in the service of the Emperor."

While Tanizaki had been the slightest bit sarcastic in uttering that platitude, Shimazo nodded quite seriously in accepting its truth. The two men sat in silence for a moment. Tanizaki glanced jealously around the Baron's gracious little home and wondered what was to become of the house and its contents. He realized suddenly that he was exceedingly glad that he wasn't the one returning to Japan. Hawaii had pulled him in; Pele, the goddess from the country beyond the sky, had conquered him. Tanizaki had been fused into the Hawaiian nation.

Shimazo began speaking again. "My mother had a wonderful trip. She was so delighted to have met you and the kids. It meant a great deal to her. She said to tell you that."

"The boys and Anne have enjoyed her company," Tanizaki responded courteously. "She shouldn't have bought them all those presents though. I don't know how we'll ever be able to repay her kindness." Really, he was quite annoyed at the generosity of the Baroness. It was too much. However *was* he to repay it?

Shimazo shook his head vigorously. "No, no," he said. "It was such a pleasure for her." His eyes touched Tanizaki's. "I think I told you before that she owns a great deal of Moritomo Industries. At her insistence, and with a considerable contribution from her, Moritomo is going to build a university in Hilo. The endowment will be large enough to make it one of the great educational institutions in the Pacific."

Tanizaki, who had drifted into his own private thoughts, came to attention at the mention of a university. If it were honestly good, then the boys could stay here and go to school. With them living at home (how he would miss them if they went away!) then there would only be the tuition...

"It's her intention not simply to have a preeminent place for scholarship, but she wants it to be free for all those born in the Hawaiian Islands." Shimazo considered his mother's plan. "I can't imagine how much that will cost!" he griped.

"Oh, really, that's kind, but she ought to leave the money to you. It's your inheritance," Tanizaki objected.

"I don't care," rebutted the Baron. "I have plenty and I

have no heirs. Still, I do think she could have set up a school somewhere in Japan..."

"Oh, but we owe the people of the territories something, surely." If the boys were able to go to a decent college here, Tanizaki wouldn't have to remain with the Imperial Police. He wasn't always quite sure that he was doing the right thing, enforcing a foreign justice on a people who had not requested it.

Tanizaki stood, eager to get on with his life. "Aloha oe," he bid Shimazo in farewell. "We'll come tomorrow to the dock and say goodbye to you and your mother."

Perry had more or less snuck up on him as he was lying in the backyard hammock having a nap. So much had happened in the last couple of days and Tanizaki was tired.

"There you are," cried Perry gleefully, waking him up.

Tanizaki came to and exhaled noisily.

"I wanted to ask a favor."

"What is it this time?"

"I wanted to borrow the Police Commander's seal from you."

Tanizaki became fully conscious and pulled himself up in the cotton sling. "What the hell are you talking about?"

"It's common knowledge on the street," Perry trumpeted. "You're the one who gave the kids the seal to use. You're the one who warned them about the raid. You're the one who got rid of Shimazo."

"He was harmless enough, really," Tanizaki argued. "I can't understand wanting to have him killed. The next Police Commander they send could be much worse."

"You saved his life."

"It wasn't me," Tanizaki denied. "What do you want the seal for anyway?"

"I wouldn't mind doing that deal with the Americans."

"Too late for that," announced Tanizaki, settling back again. "Moritomo Industries took the matter into its own hands. It's formed a joint venture with the Americans to develop the

Oahu beachfront. Moritomo land and American money. They'll reconstruct the whole damn island as a resort. Let's hope to Pele they don't start side junkets to the Big Island."

In the year 2003, the Islands were ceded back to the Hawaiian people by an indifferent Imperial Japanese government. The latest cabinet wanted to rid itself of the drain of maintaining far-flung colonies.

The Fusion Party dominated the first Hawaiian Congress. Takeo Tanizaki, a former Police Inspector–currently a real estate agent on the Big Island–was elected to represent his predominantly Polynesian district on the Fusion ticket. He was a popular politician and spoke three of the languages of the Islands.

One of the voters was asked at an exit poll for whom she had cast her ballot.

"Tanizaki," she replied in satisfaction.

"Why would you vote for a Japanese, the former oppressor?"

"He's not Japanese," the woman disagreed with a perplexed frown. "Though maybe by extraction. He's quite laid back. you see. Very Polynesian. I saw him on the television." Television had come to the Islands a few years before. "Very Aloha." She meant "way Fusion," of course.

Tanizaki watched this exchange on a TV in the bar where he was drinking a beer with his brother-in-law and waiting for his wife. He laughed. Next week he and Anne were flying to San Francisco on vacation. His old boss, Baron Shimazo, was living there now, heading the Japanese West Coast Consulate. Of course the Tanizakis would visit him there.

Shimazo was a cousin, after all.

About the Author

A long-time trade journalist, G. Miki Hayden has written about everything from supercomputers, to corporate security, to health care. The author's previously published fiction includes stories in several genres.